Six spooky tales written & illustrated by
Rylan John Cavell

& Other Stories   Rylan John Cavell

& Other Stories

Rylan John Cavell

THE BLOOD MOON
AND OTHER STORIES

The Blood Moon

The young girl filled her basket with meat and bread and wine and cheese, packing it tightly about with fabric. She dressed well against the weather outside in a thick skirt, woollen gloves, sturdy boots and her favourite cap and cloak.

Her mother reminded her that at this time of year the sun set early, and that she must not stray from the path through the woods. Dangerous men and strange ladies and odd creatures, or worse, oozed and scurried and strolled and paraded through the deep woods at night. The girl kissed her mother on the cheek, promising to travel true and straight upon the path, and not to stray.

"Grandmama is expecting you, Blanchette, and has a bed made up for you to stay with her in the cottage." Her mother said, fussing at her daughter's clothes, "You must be sure to be well behaved and make her a filling breakfast in the morning before returning home."

The girl nodded and brushed off her mother's cautions and worry.

"I will be quite fine." Said she, "I know the way and the light is good for several hours yet."

She set off with a merry spring in her step from the village and along the path towards the woods, on the other side of which lay her Grandmother's home. She held her basket firm and skipped happily in the late afternoon sun. Birds sang cheerful ditties, rabbits hurried to their holes as she passed, and the world was still lush and green. The colours of autumn were yet to creep into the leaves of the wood or upon the plants growing in the gardens and farmsteads of the village.

From ahead of her there came the rhythmic sound of an axe hitting wood.

Blanchette's father was employed in the maintenance of the woods, and was currently at the scrubby edge of that dark and tangled place. He ensured that it did not encroach too close to the village, providing households with firewood and carpenters with their raw materials.

He waved to his daughter, and she went over to say her farewells. He was grave and leaned on his axe as he too warned her not to stray from the path, and travel straight to her Grandmother's house where she was expected. Once more Blanchette assuaged her parent's fears. She was a wilful and strong minded girl, and did not see why she should be so fussed over when embarking on a journey she had made time and time before.

"Tonight is a rare night," Her father said sternly, "The moon will turn red, and vile creatures will be let loose of their bonds to stalk the lands. You must go straight to Grandmama's cottage. There you will be safe. Do not stray."

His severity was unusual, but Blanchette smiled and kissed him upon the cheek.

"I will be quite safe." Said she, and skipped back to the path and into the woods.

Just inside the line of the trees she paused to wave at her Father, who stood watching her go. He waved back,

9

took up his axe and returned to his felling of a dead and broken Yew tree.

Sunlight did not much penetrate the thick layers of foliage that formed the cathedral-like domes and spires of the woodland canopy. Trunks of trees, both thick and thin, straight and bent stood each side of the path. Looking to either left or right gave no more of a view than the other, as the trees were crowded so tightly together that you could only see a few feet in any direction.

Blanchette knew that the path was winding and little more than a rut in the ground made deep by many years of intrepid feet moving from one side of the wood to another. She also knew the route well, and so her mind wandered as her feet took control and led the way.

She dwelt upon her father's words. What had he meant about the moon turning red? It was likely to be some daft superstition only the grown ups of the village believed. She did not think the moon could change its colour. It did not wear a gown of white, that now and again was exchanged for another in burgundy. It was a silly notion, and she laughed quietly to herself thinking how remarkable it was for her father, a man so strapping and strong and fearless, should be made to shiver upon thinking of the moon! She didn't think her father could be afraid of anything.

Presently she came upon the half-way point of her journey through the woods, a place she knew well. A wide pool of still water lay beside the path, fed by a narrow brook that burbled softly over rocks and roots. Here, where the trees parted to allow the water room to stretch, the sky was visible, and a single shaft of light angled across the pool.

Blanchette decided to rest a while, and to enjoy the warmth of the sun upon her face. She sat at the side of the path, watching motes of light glint and dance in the air.

"Hello there," Said a wolf, peering through the darkness.

Blanchette was startled by its voice and could not see from whence it approached. Something upon the water caught her eye, and she thought she might have caught a glimpse of the animal's shaggy reflection.

"Hello there." Said she, sure that she was in no danger, as she had never seen a wolf before, and knew not their reputation for savagery and their hunger for flesh.

"What are you doing alone in the woods?"

"I am on my way to visit Grandmama. I am taking her food and wine for she is old and frail. A hearty dinner and plentiful breakfast will do her a power of good and fortify her a little ahead of the winter months."

The wolf's green eyes glinted, peering out across the pool of still water.

"Do not hurry." It said, "There is so much to see in the woods! Such pretty flowers, the like of which you will never have known; that grow and glow in the darkness beneath these trees."

Blanchette shook her head, standing up and clutching her basket tightly.

"I'm sure they are delightful, but I must be on my way. Good bye."

And on she went, a quickness in her step now, as she did not want to remain in the woods too long. Grandmama was waiting, after all.

The woods began eventually to thin, and open up above Blanchette to reveal a darkening sky. Clouds were collected overhead, promising rain. The young girl hurried to her Grandmother's door and knocked. Presently the door was opened and her Grandmother welcomed her joyously inside. They hugged and they kissed each other on the cheek, and Blanchette showed the old woman what she had in her basket.

Grandmama was most pleased with the package of food and wine, and pleased more so that Blanchette had made it to her before the fall of night.

"Why is everyone so suddenly scared by night time?" She asked of her Grandmother, "Mother, and Father, and you all warned me to be here by nightfall."

Grandmama stroked Blanchette's yellow hair, "It is not night we fear, but the companions at her heel. Especially on a night like tonight."

"The red moon?"

"They call it the Blood Moon."

Grandmama and Blanchette ate well of meat and cheese and bread, and the old woman allowed herself a small glass of wine.

"It's medicinal, of course."

And as the sun hid its face, so Grandmama prepared for bed. She bolted the windows and doors, and

12

stoked the fire so that it might last a while longer untended.

"This is your bed, my dearest little one." Said Grandmama of the odd fabric box in the corner of the room.

It seemed to be a miniature four poster bed, draped on all sides with curtains, so that you could not see inside, or when within, could not see out.

Blanchette, ready for sleep and to be cosy, crawled into her bed and kissed Grandmama good night. The old woman appeared wistful and distant, nodding and wishing the girl sweet dreams.

The curtained side through which she had climbed was closed, and Blanchette was lost in darkness. The fabric draped on all sides was thick and heavy. She did not wish to be in such pitch black as yet. She was tired, but not *that* tired and wished to stay awake and watch the fire slowly dwindle in the hearth as she herself dwindled from wakefulness to sleep.

Reaching out a hand to push back a curtain, her fingers fell upon something she did not expect. Thin metal bars stood rigid around her. A lattice of metalwork stood on every side, and she pulled at it, unsure as to why there should be a cage around her bed.

"Hush, dear. Please do not struggle."

Grandmama's voice was quiet and wavering. She sounded like she may be weeping.

Blanchette managed to grab at the curtain on one side of her through the bars, and pulled at it hard. It came away at the top, falling to the ground. Now she could see that this was no bed, it was an animal's cage, lined with fabric and a small mattress and pillows.

Through the bolted cottage windows an ill red light filled the room. It was a feverish illumination, and it made the young girl feel sick to her stomach. She asked her Grandmother why she was trapped in this cage, to which the old woman looked away, unable to keep her eyes upon Blanchette.

Fumbling through the bars of the bed cage, the young girl found a latch, and set herself free. The metalwork clanged loudly as it hit the ground, and she jumped out into the room.

Her Grandmother screamed and held up her arms, backing away from the girl in abject horror.

"What's the matter Grandmama?" Blanchette demanded, "What do you fear?"

The old woman backed away across the room toward the fire, where she grabbed up the poker, and held it out in front of her as a weapon.

"Look upon the mirror." Her voice cracked and warbled, broken by fear.

Confused and upset, Blanchette did as she was bid. She looked to the mirror which hung on the wall, and did not understand what she saw.

There was no Blanchette standing there. In her place stood a starling, wire-haired, green eyed beast.

"You are a wolf!"

"How can this be?" Asked the girl, as the world she thought she knew fell apart, "How am I a wolf?"

"Keep back!" Grandmama jabbed with the poker, catching Banchette across one shoulder.

She whimpered and took a step away, then an anger and a hunger rose up from deep in her gut. It was new and unfamiliar and it overtook her senses as night overtakes day.

"You hurt me!" Blanchette admonished Grandmama angrily, and pounced.

Long teeth tore into thin limbs. Dark claws pulled at clothes and hair. Under the sickly light of the Blood Moon, Grandmama's blood pooled black as tar.

Blanchette did not remember how she found her way home, or how long she had been travelling lost in the woods.

Her Mother and Father were stricken with panic at her arrival at their front door.

"You have been gone for three days!" Her Mother wailed.

Her Father asked her why she wore only her cap and cloak, why she was naked as the day she was born. He asked her how she had become so dirtied, and why there was dried blood upon her lips.

Blanchette gently shook her head, unable to recall precisely the details of the previous few days.

"I went to visit Grandmama," She recounted foggily, "But there was a wolf."

"Indeed there was a wolf." Her Father agreed, hefting his axe upon his shoulder.

Blanchette's Mother began to weep, and it distressed Blanchette to her very core.

"Please do not cry. I'm sure that all will be well. We can visit Grandmama together if you wish." Said she.

"Come with me." Said her Father, opening the door to their home and stepping outside.

Blanchette followed her father in silence along the path from the village to the edge of the woods.

"Where are we going?" She asked.

Her Father did not reply, but led her deeper and deeper along the path.

Presently, birds took to the air in fright as a brief and shrill scream was silenced by the thick and heavy thud of an axe.

THE END

Sally Rattles

PART ONE

She blew in on a westerly wind, clutching a
tattered and broken umbrella like her life depended on it.
Slumping amongst the crates and boxes at the docks, she
hoped to go unnoticed by the workers, loading ships bound
for exotic and colourful lands far overseas. She found a
crate marked rum, and thought to herself 'don't mind if I
do.' A short while later, intoxicated, and singing a lewd
song, she made herself known to the Master of the Docks,
who attempted to move her on.

"Come along now, strange Miss, on your way."

But she would not be on her way, and insisted upon
telling the man about how she came to be in such a sorry
state.

"I really don't think I care." Said he, before
noticing her wince, and seeing a thick stain of blood on her
clothing, slick and wet on her belly.
He shouted for someone to fetch a Doctor, as she slumped,
slurring to the floor,

"You wouldn't believe it 'less you saw it for
yourself."

Some indeterminate number of weeks previously, a
Nanny quit her job, strode huffily to a waiting carriage, and
berated the Maid who clung to her coat sleeve and who
begged her to stay. The household of which she had had her
fill was that of the Gutters, at 17 Spindle Street. It was a
very wealthy district of the city of London, though as it is
often said; money cannot buy happiness. The tall pale
facades of the buildings regularly turned blind curtained
eyes from the events at Number 17. The young Gutterlings;

Agnes and Thomas were prone to ill behaviour and bad
temper, often running away from home to play with kites
and stray dogs in the park at the end of the road. They
cared not for bed time, washing behind their ears, keeping
their elbows off the table, or maintaining a tidy Nursery.

"What about the children?" implored the Maid,

"The children ...?... are gone! Again!" The exiting
Nanny shrieked, shaking with rage as she was driven away.

No sooner was the Nanny out of sight, Mrs Gutter
swept up to and into the house, her mascara stained in
dried tearful streaks down her face. This would not be an
uncommon sight, aside from the Police Constable who had
escorted her roughly home. Mrs Gutter clutched her sash,
in the colours of the Suffragettes, though it was torn, as it
had been ripped from her earlier in the day.

"Unhand me!" She cried out, once within the safety
and confidence of her own home.

She was all sinew and tendon, pulled tight like the
ligaments in the leg of a race horse. The Constable
dismissed himself from his escort duties as Mr Gutter
returned home. By contrast to his wife, the Master of the
house was loose and gelatinous and could be painted as a
landscape. He wore his suit too tight, which often caused
an alarming reddening of his cheeks, as parts of his large
form tried to break free from within the tight and
restraining collar and cuffs. The sight of the departing
constable caused a considerable rouge to bolster the already
blotchy tone of his skin.

Mr and Mrs Gutter fought. They fought often. He shouted and she shouted, and he banged his fist and she wailed and all the while neither of them ever truly listened to what the other was saying. They spoke their minds, and said their piece, and spat out words like weapons. Their defence, both of them, was to become impervious to the emotions of the other, so nothing ever improved their situation, and they did not learn or mature or grow, and the light of their love which had once burned bright as the sun flickered and diminished and became the memory of embers.

Happy and ignorant of today's vocal battle, Agnes and Thomas returned home, laughing and cavorting and with their clothes covered in mud and torn at the knee. Mr Gutter called out for the Nanny. But she did not come. In place of the absent Nanny, Mr Gutter took discipline into his own hands, striking both his children with an open palm. They were shocked to immobility and silence.

"Go to the nursery." He then said to them, in a low growl, "Bathe and to bed. At once."

Mrs Gutter and the Maid took the stunned children away upstairs in a careful hurry. In the quiet of the vast rooms of 17 Spindle Street, Mr Gutter took up a pen and paper to write an advertisement for a new Governess.

"Clearly I have left the hiring of Nannies to the women for too long." Said he, "I shall write this advertisement. I shall interview the applicants. I shall be the judge of who will best care for my children, as clearly only I am capable of such a feat. They want sugar. It is time for salt."

Days later and the advert had been well received. A line of sour-faced spinsters and widows made a crooked and hunched line to the door of number 17 Spindle Street. The day was overcast, and grey clouds swirled about each other in a mockery of dance. As the wind whipped at the thick skirts of the women who would be Nannies, a foul smell came with it. The crones and grannies sniffed and squinted and pouted their lips in distaste. Coming along the road behind them, singing a lewd song, swinging an umbrella as a conductor does a baton, a young woman of no fixed abode approached. Her clothes were once very fine, but age and the passing down from person to person had made them dull, frayed in places and discoloured in others. She joined the back of the queue, finishing her song suddenly very quietly into the ear of the nearest woman.

"Excuse me!" Remarked the biddy.

"Why? What have you done?" Asked the dishevelled damsel.

By smell, and by rudeness, and by crudeness, and by harassment she created disturbances enough to make the line of women dwindle. They one by one departed, grumbling that no job was worth this harassment.

The woman leaned her elbow upon the shoulder of the nearest elderly old dear, resting her weight there as she removed one of her shoes to scratch between her toes. The smell, it seemed, was emanating from these well-worn and paper-thin articles. It was the aroma of forgotten vinegar and blue cheese that would easily peel wallpaper. The old dear covered her mouth and nose with a handkerchief.

"I'm Sally by the way. What're you all waiting for?" Said the urchin, satisfied that the itch between her toes had been satiated she replaced her shoe.

The old dear began to speak, was almost sick into her handkerchief, then hurried away.

"I thought this was a reputable area." Sniffed the next waiting would-be employee, "Clearly not, if you are common in these parts."

"Lovey, all my parts are common." Sally laughed, prodding the stuffy older woman with her umbrella.

"The impudence!" She scoffed as she too decided to depart the queue.

"I could really do with a piss." Sally was hopping slightly, clenching her thighs together, "Is there a lav at the end of this line?"

As they waited, Sally attempted to engage the next woman in conversation. This woman tried to ignore the scruffy person at her ear until a wet trickling sound began during a break in the chatter. Looking down, the woman noticed a delicate stream of yellow liquid creating a spreading, steaming pool around and under her shoes.

"Sorry." Sally said as she stood from a squatted position, "Did I get some on you?"

Disgusted, the remainder of the women tutted and made swift exits.

The odorous newcomer laughed and leant against the metal railings of the house by which she stood.

"I wonder what they were waiting for."

Behind her, the Maid beckoned her inside, "Are you the only one?"

"Only one what?"

"Name?" Demanded Mr Gutter.

"Sally Rattles."

The young woman was shown from the front door and toward the drawing room. Hurrying across the hall, Thomas had dared to pilfer a snack of a thick ham and cheese sandwich from the kitchen. Sally's hungry eyes spotted the food, and without pause for thought, snatched it from the boy's hands.

"Hey!" He protested loudly.

Mr Gutter turned on his heel at the sound of his son's voice, and was about to bellow at the boy... But he didn't have to. A cat-like hiss from Sally, and a fake toward him sent Thomas scuttling backward from her and up the stairs with his tail between his legs.

Mr Gutter regarded the tatty woman as she slowly took a huge bite of the sandwich.

"What?" She said, spitting crumbs.

She was put onto a small wooden chair in the centre of the large drawing room, around which Mr Gutter was pacing, while making notes in a black pocket book. He did not care to look up at her, for he had made his decision.

"What a grand house this is." She remarked quietly to herself. "Never been in one this size before. Madame Flinching's was a good size, having to house six of us girls an' all, but not as fancy as all this."

Mr Gutter took a deep breath and began to recite his pre prepared interview speech.

"What I am looking for is someone of the most flexible nature. Able to meet with anything I may thrust at her." Mr Gutter punctuated the word *thrust* with a jab of his pen in her direction.

Sally scratched at her chin, trying to remember through clouds of gin addled memories where exactly she had seen his face before. She continued to eat the sandwich, brushing crumbs onto the floor from her lap.

"I need a woman who knows how to be strict, yet how to be soft." Said he.

"I remember you. Never had you pegged for living in a fancy pad like this'n."

"Mine are a handful, and so need some very special attention. I expect reports of their behaviour regularly."

Sally shrugged, finishing the sandwich,
"Not been in the game for a while. Trying to go straight, as they say."

Then she thought *'Still, a John's a John at the end of the day. No matter what the wrapping, it's still the same old battered sausage and chips inside.'*

"They are the future. They shall grow up into a world forged by British workmanship and determination. But they need careful guidance. They are to be the beating heart and organs, pumping the lifeblood of commerce and trade around this mighty Empire of ours." Mr Gutter had clearly rehearsed several passages of his monologue, and was so focussed on the drama of his words that he was not listening to Sally's replies.

24

"If only they could see me now, talking to a posh bloke like this! I suppose I could fall back on my old tricks for a few bob."

"However, at present this household, like a ship at sea with no map, is somewhat adrift."

Now Mr Gutter stopped his pacing and looked once more at Sally Rattles. He did not like her clothes, or the smell of her that was slowly seeping into his awareness, but he would easily purchase her some suitable and sensible items for the commencement of her employ.

"Nothing too kinky though. Don't mind a quick wash-up after, but if I have to scrub you've gone too far."

Lost in thoughts of helping to dress Sally, he continued to hear what he wanted to, and not the words she uttered, "I need a firm hand to take hold of the rudder, while I attempt to steer us toward safety. If you believe yourself to be the level-headed and eager woman that I need then sign here on the dotted line, and head upstairs immediately to begin your work."

More than a little bit confused, Sally signed an X on the paperwork held to her, and was taken upstairs by the Maid. Her confusion escalated further when she was shown into the Nursery.

Agnes and Thomas froze when she entered the room.

"I don't think I was listening properly. What am I here for? What did I sign?"

"Where's my sandwich?" Thomas demanded.

A flicker of Sally's eyelid was enough to send the boy diving onto his bed and under the covers like a tortoise into its shell.

"They're your problem now." Said the Maid, strangely smug.

"Terrific." Sally said, as the Maid left, closing the door behind her.

She turned back around to face the children and their Nursery. Everything was a shade of cream. The room had been bleached of all personality. Even the toys were painted pastel shades of chalk and light beige. It was the least stimulating room Sally has ever had the misfortune to find herself in. The room was also a mess. Not just a little bit 'lived in', but utterly disorganised. There were clothes forming a steep mountainside into the depths of the wardrobe, the rocking horse was laid on its side, and the dolls house had disgorged tiny furniture across the floor. Here and there food stains and peculiar smears were bright and colourful, almost pleasing to the eye amongst the bland sterility of the room. Sally noticed a single sock hanging from a lamp sconce above one of the beds.

"What are you looking at?" Agnes snapped.

Sally's patented 'scare stare' had seemingly little effect on the girl, but Thomas, who had begun to peep from under the covers with one eye, swiftly returned to hiding.

"Are you our new Nanny?" He asked from his fortress of duck down.

Sally chewed upon her response for a moment, or was it a bit of ham stuck between her teeth?

"I think so."

She reached a dirty finger into the recesses of her mouth to pluck out the offending item.

"You don't look like a Nanny." Agnes folded her arms, leaning against the soot-smeared fire surround.

Sally found the niggling ham and prized it free.

"You look like a tavern wench!" The girl finished, clearly thinking the insult would cut Sally deeply. Sally stared at the ham on her fingertip, before casually flicking it at Agnes.

"How do you know what one of them looks like, prissy missy?"

Agnes gasped as the ham landed on her blouse. She leaped around the room, shaking and squealing as if bitten by some nightmarish insect.

Sally rolled her eyes, and began to take off her coat. She hung it, along with her umbrella on the back of the Nursery door. By the time she had straightened out her clothes, and turned back around to face the children, Agnes had stopped her flailing, and Thomas was suppressing laughter.

"You're so common." Once more Agnes attempted to insult her new Nanny.

"Even posh folk become common, when there's enough of 'em about the place."

Sally pondered what a Nanny might do in this situation. Unruly children in an unruly Nursery. At least one of those things she could set to work on at once.

"Right, you two 'orrible oiks, guess what?" She grinned, displaying an almost complete set of front teeth.

Thomas dared to poke his head above his parapet of pillows, "What?"

"We're going to tidy this room."

Agnes and Thomas both groaned.

"Come along," Sally clapped her hands together, "A job well begun is half done. Or some similar such bollocks."

Thomas gasped, "You swore!"

"If you get off your arse and tidy this room," Sally said, thinking quickly, "I'll give you some sweets."

This got the attention of both children, and they began to tidy under Sally's direction. Unwilling though they both were to take much of an active part in the neatening and fussing of the room, the promise of sweets drove them on to complete the task.

"Can we have our sweets yet?" Thomas moaned, as he tried to force the wardrobe doors closed over the cascade of unhung clothes.

"Not on your nelly!"

After a great deal of nagging and goading, and reissuing of the promise of confectionery, the children finally had a tidy Nursery. They sat up eagerly, yet warily, on the end of their beds, watching Sally inspect the room.

Sally made a show of eyeballing the Nursery from top to bottom, running a finger along surfaces to check for dust. Finally Sally agreed that they had done a good enough job to warrant sweets.

"But you'll not get them until tomorrow." She said firmly.

"No!" Wailed Thomas, "That's not fair. We tidied everything!"

"You told us we could have sweets if we tidied the Nursery!" Agnes gritted her teeth.

"Didn't say when you'd get them though, did I? Didn't specify, did I? You just assumed, didn't you? That's my first lesson to you as your Nanny. Life's hard. It's unfair. It's full of shit people and shittier situations. If you're lucky, fate might deal you an unexpected hand. Make the most of it, whatever it is."

The children stared at her with open mouths.

"Shut your traps. You look like fish on a market stall."

Sally did not wait for the Children to reply or to obey her command. She left the Nursery, taking her coat and umbrella with her, and descended the stairs, hunting out some member of the household. The Maid was the first person she found.

"Oi, you." Said Sally.

The Maid froze, eyes wide, afraid that Sally might offer a protest about the children and make to leave already, "Yes?"

"Do I get a room in this old heap, or what?"

Sally did indeed get a room in the 'old heap'. It was little more than a cupboard in size and was in the eaves so she bumped her head now and again on the beams of the roof, but it was cosy. There was a small bath and wash basin in the room, and several thin sheets under a crocheted blanket on the single bed. Compared to other places Sally had called home, this was luxury. She ran her hands over the blanket on the bed. It was rough and scratchy, but to

29

her it was akin to the finest of Chinese silks. She smiled to herself, and moved to clean a small square mirror which hung on the back of the door. Her grubby reflection stuck its tongue out at her, and she chuckled.

"Talk about landing on your feet, my girl." She said to the Sally in the little mirror.

A short while later she had herself a shallow lukewarm bath run. In it she sat, happily sloshing water and soap bubbles over herself as thoroughly as she was able. It was not a large tub, and her knees were up near her nose, but this cleansing of the body was a luxurious self-indulgence she was able to partake of so infrequently she didn't mind the tight fit of the bath around her buttocks.

As she dried herself, there came a knock at the door.

"What?" Sally called out.

"Sally Rattles?"

It was Mr Gutter at the door to her room. It was unheard of for the Master of the house to visit the servant's quarters. Luckily Sally had had the foresight to lock the door during her bath, and the key was still snug in the lock.

"What do you want?" Said she.

"Your working attire. I have it. Would you open the door?"

Sally was cautious, "Just leave it outside. I'm not decent."

"Miss Rattles, open the door."

"Not on your nelly. Leave the clothes out there, then bugger off."

There followed the sound of Mr Gutter attempting to start a number of sentences, or one sentence several different ways. Whatever he wanted to say, it would not come out, or he could not bring himself to say it.

"What's that you're saying?" Sally moved closer to the door to better hear his flustered mumbles.

He didn't say anything else. A few creaky floorboards later, and Sally understood that he had descended the stairs and was gone elsewhere in the house. She unlocked the door and poked her head out, finding that he had indeed left a parcel wrapped in brown paper on the floor. Sally grabbed it up quickly and slammed the door shut again.

"Who wants to go to the park?" Sally asked loudly as she burst into the Nursery.

Agnes and Thomas were once again taken by surprise by her entrance, and now also by her remarkably different appearance. She wore a very smart dress and jacket in navy blue, and there was a small black straw hat perched on her hair, held in place by a gleaming silver hat pin.

"Sally?" Thomas asked, "Is that you?"

"Course it's me. Just had a wash, that's all." Sally grinned.

Agnes sneered, "You can't scrub away *common*. That stink will linger on you for life."

Sally grabbed the young girl by the ear and twisted, hard. Agnes cried out in shock and in pain. Never had a Nanny laid a hand on her like this before!

"Would you like to keep a matching set?" Sally said sweetly, still twisting the ear.

"Let go!" Agnes tried to hit out at Sally, but each of her blows was batted away easily.

"Hmm?" Sally grabbed Agnes' other ear now as well.

"I'm sorry!" Agnes began to cry, tears erupting like a geyser from her eyes, screwed up tight.

Sally let go of the girls ears, and nodded happily. "That'll do."

Agnes clutched at her ears and hurried to the far side of the room, ensuring there were plenty of obstacles between herself and her assailant. Sally did not chase her, or shout, or scold her.

"I said," Sally paused, waiting for Agnes' sobbing to subside, "Who wants to go to the park?"

Swaddled in coats and scarfs and hats, Sally led Thomas and Agnes from the heavy black front door of 17 Spindle Street.

"Can we please get some sweets while we are out?" Thomas asked, needling Sally about the reward for tidying the Nursery which had yet to be forthcoming.

"If you're good."

Sally was beginning to like Thomas, and in return Thomas seemed to be liking her. Boundaries had been set early on, and the boy was smart enough to know not to push at them too hard.

"You can't change the conditions of the promise now." Agnes snorted, "We tidied the Nursery, that was enough. Now we have to be good *as well*?"

Agnes was another matter altogether. Sally shot the girl a sideways look, and her hands protectively shot up to her ears for fear of another severe twisting. Sally wondered why Agnes was so determined to be a pain in her backside. Clearly the girl required some form of extra attention, but as she was only three hours into this job, Sally was flummoxed as to what to do about her.

"I'll work you out. Puzzlebox girl." Sally murmured out loud.

"What?"

"Nothing." Sally cleared her throat, "Now then. Where's the park from here? I only ever went at night."

Thomas took hold of Sally's hand and led the way, with Agnes trailing behind.

The park was large and sprawling, with manicured lawns and well tended hedge mazes. A few enclosures survived from an earlier time where the park had been a sprawling zoo. Now only a handful of animals remained, weary and wearing glazed expressions. The park gates were ornate iron, curled around and around like ivy. They stood open, allowing people of all social standing to wander in and enjoy a sweet and calming few minutes in a neat and tidy green oasis, before once more heading out into the grey and brown smudges of the city of London.

A hunched shape came ambling out of the park just as Sally, Thomas and Agnes arrived there. This hunched shape was a wizened man, who's years were not as advanced as they looked. He wore his face loosely, his hair was unkempt, and beneath his heavy cloak was a suit which had once cost a great deal of money.

"Oh no." Sallly Rattles' face lost all colour at the sight of him, and she froze to the spot.

"What is it?" Agnes asked, following Sally's gaze.

"Well do my eyes deceive me, or do I spy one Sally Rattles?"

The hunched figure stood more erect, holding his arms wide, so that as his cloak expanded over his thin limbs it gave the appearance of a cobra rising and fanning out its neck.

"Afternoon Ron." Sally said, pushing herself to appear calm and collected.

She couldn't freeze up. She wouldn't let herself be intimidated by him. Not any more.

"And who might these little tykes belong to?"

"I'm their Nanny." Sally said, attempting to sidestep his question as neatly as possible.

"Why are you talking to this... person?" Agnes said, feeling slightly braver now that Sally had unfrozen.

The crooked man moved forward, holding out a hand to shake that of the young girl. His hand remained empty.

"They call me Old Ron," He introduced himself, "Pleased to make your acquaintance, young lady. Precious little thing like you, out and about with only Miss Rattles for protection. Why, anything might happen."

34

Sally squared her shoulders, "Ron." She said gravely, as a warning.

"Did they even call you *Old* Ron when you were young?" Thomas asked, but Agnes shushed him.

Ron aimed his long nose and small eyes back up to Sally.

"I've not seen you since, oh when was it? Oh yes, since I reminded you of how much you owed me."
"I don't owe you *anything*." Sally clenched her jaw, her mind ticking over quickly, planning an escape route for herself and her young wards.

Ron was not usually in and of himself a dangerous man. He was not strong of limb, but his mind was sharp and dripped with venom. His contacts and influence spread far and wide through the underworld of London akin to a fungus through the floor of a forest.

Ron's little eyes flicked curiously across the children. He was sizing them up, taking in the details of their clothes and skin, their posture and the angles of their faces.

"I've cleaned chimneys up and down and across the whole of London. There's not a family or its secrets I don't know. You, boy. What's your name?" Ron jabbed a crooked finger at Thomas.

Before Sally could silence him, Thomas offered his first name.

Ron played his tongue around his teeth in thought. A little boy called Thomas, an older sister who looks to have seen the back of someone's hand in recent days. These observations, combined with his esoteric wisdom, he calculated exactly who they were.

"You're the Gutters, aren't you?"

Thomas nodded. Agnes simply stared at him, her face still and difficult to read.

"Swept your chimneys two months back."

"That's when the silver went missing." Agnes whispered to Thomas, indicating with an exaggerated look at Old Ron who she now thought may have been responsible.

"A man in my position takes the opportunities what come his way." Ron grinned, showing off his thin, peg-like teeth, "Where you been Sally? What you been filling your time with? It's been months."

Step by step Sally had been nudging the children and herself in an arc, attempting to pass Ron and escape into the throngs in the park. Ron was not daft, and he matched their movements with his own small shuffling steps.

"Trying to stay clean, and clear of you. If you must know." Sally said, giving up on trying to bypass the old man.

He reached into a pocket and held out a paper bag to her, "So you wouldn't be interested in any of these?"

Thomas' curiosity overtook him, and he reached out and took hold of the bag.

"Sweets?" He asked.

Sally snatches the bag away from the boy, tossing it back to Ron.

"I told you. Clean." She spat, her anger and fear now visible for all to see.

Ron lurched forward, taking hold of Sally's hair and pulling her around to face the children. They both gasped and clutched onto the other as Ron palmed a slim dagger from his sleeve and held it up at Sally's throat. The keen edge bit her skin and a small bead of rich red liquid began to appear.

"You fucking bitch." Ron's venom was audible, "You dare run away from me? After all I did for you?"

The paper bag lay on the floor. Ron nodded to it and instructed Thomas to pick it up.

"Eat what's inside." He instructed, "Or we say tatty bye to Miss Rattles. You too, girl."

They faltered, unsure what to do. The genteel folk passing to and fro scattered. Heaven forbid they should get involved in the antics of street ruffians. Someone called out for the police, but no constables were within earshot.

Ron adjusted his hold on Sally and the knife, causing a trail of blood to begin trickling down her neck.

"Why should we?" Agnes attempted bravery.

"Sally would look ever so different without a head, wouldn't she?" Ron laughed.

Thomas pulled on Agnes' sleeve, "Please, I don't want her to get stabbed."

There were tears in his eyes, panic in his voice, and a small trickle of urine running down the inside of his left leg.

Agnes did not back down, "We'll just go home. We'll tell Mother and Father she ran away."

"Please..." Sally whispered, her eyes wide.

No man had ever instilled fear in her like Old Ron. He wielded fear and his unsettling presence with more deadly accuracy than any weapon.

Thomas pulled items from the paper bag and ate them. Agnes was torn, but reluctantly gave in, and followed her brother's example.

Ron spun Sally away, snatching back the paper bag at the same time. He took a handful and ate, then offered the bag to Sally, who shook her head.

"I want to go home." Thomas said in a small voice, "I don't feel very well."

Sally wiped at the blood on her neck, pulling her colour up to hide the small wound.

"No no, my boy." Ron grinned, little bubbles of spit forming at the side of his mouth, "We're off on an adventure!"

Sally knelt in front of the children, pulling their attention to her. She forced a smile, and put on a brave voice.

"Think happy thoughts Agnes, Thomas. Let's hurry into the park. Let's go and see the animals at the zoo."

Clutching their hands tightly, Sally pulled them after her into the park.

Thomas looked to his sister, and gasped at what he saw. Her pale skin seemed to be glowing, and her blue eyes appeared twice their normal size. Around him shapes began to blur as the green of the plants and many speckled highlights of flowers started to gain a new and electric vibrancy.

The maze was tipped with leaves like hands,
That waved at him from on high.
He skipped through these miraculous lands,
And wished that he could fly.
The flowers spoke, and sang strange songs, and winked as he passed through.
The towers broke, and chimed their gongs, and said they hadn't a clue.

Right past the gypsy woman, hunched like a hill,
And over the bridge 'cross the stream.
Left past the dancer, with movement to thrill,
And around in this tangled half dream.
The green walls grew taller, made streaks of the sky, thin blue lines high above.
The grey ground shrank smaller, 'I am lost' he did cry, but this world held him snug in kid glove.

     Sally chased Thomas through the hedge maze. Both children had slipped her grasp and made off in different directions, following whatever delight they believed they saw. The boy's laughter wove between the tall hedges of the maze and the well maintained flower beds that dotted small open areas amongst the tangle. This way and another she wound, hurrying past others, equally or even more lost than her. After quite long enough of following the paths of the maze, she decided to take matters into her own hands and make her own path. She pushed her way through the hedge wall and into another green corridor. Then another. Then another. Twigs stole her hat. Leaves found their way into her sleeves.

"Fuck sake!" Sally shouted, causing a canoodling young couple to run away in shock.

Thomas, giggling and with eyes focussed on nothing, rounded the corner past the retreating couple. Sally wasted no time in snatching him up and dragging him back through her path of destruction out of the maze.

And the penguins danced the polka as the monkeys sang their woes,
The giraffe whispered a ditty and lamented her lack of toes.
'What use is a tail, with no trees on which to climb?'
A local cat stalked softly by, its little bell to chime.

'A hoof! A hoof! What good is a hoof?
I want to dance, and twirl and prance, and whirl in the finest floof!'
'With flippers; two, who can serve tea?
Not we! Not we! Not we!'

And the monkeys wrote a sonnet as the penguins served them cake,
Confectionary made with a friendly grin by the crocodile in the lake.
'A cup of sugar and a turquoise egg, then mix it with a spoon.'
The local cat stretched out her claws and said 'you are a loon.'

The cat went on stalking and observing while mute,
Penguins took to water and flamingo played the flute.
So the giraffe danced in ballet as the monkeys spoke aloud that;
'Every silver lining must indeed have a cloud.'

"Agnes!"

Sally shouted, stunned by what she saw. People were running in panic in all directions as the animals from the zoo enclosures trotted and galloped and waddled out of their cages and pens. Agnes sat amongst them all, miming pouring tea from a pot into a cup, and handing it to a penguin, who watched her with one beady black eye. It pecked at her fingers.

"Don't snatch." Agnes scolded the penguin.

It hooted; high pitched and shrill, flapped its flightless wings, and scurried away to join its friends. Somewhere nearby a monkey threw droppings at a woman in a wide feathered hat.

Taking hold of Agnes by her collar, Sally yanked her abruptly from the imaginary animalian tea party.

A narrow woman draped in the remains of a shawl slowly made her way across the park, a flock of pigeons hopping and fluttering and strutting around her.

"Breadcrumbs. Penny a beg." She muttered to anyone who dared pass closely by her, "Feed the birds?"

The afternoon waned swiftly into evening. The moon slunk up greasily behind thick and angry clouds as Agnes and Thomas, washed, changed and put to bed were recovering from their strange experiences at the park. Thomas held his head, and Agnes looked ready to vomit for the Nth time since arriving home.

"I think my brain is broken." Thomas groaned as he lay heavily back onto his pillows.

Agnes gulped down something which threatened to escape her bowls, complexion a pale shade of pea green.

"That man Ron was horrid. What do you owe him?"

Sally shushed away the question, instead fussing at the covers, tucking the children into their comfortable beds.

"Why did he want to stab you?" Thomas asked.

Sally burst out, slightly louder than she intended, that she did not wish to speak of it. Not now, and not any time soon, thank you very much you nosey oiks!

Thomas took hold of her hands as she passed him in her fussing,

"I didn't want him to stab you. I think you're strange, and you smell weird... but I don't want anyone to stab you. It's not very nice."

Sally released a breath she had held onto too tightly. She deflated, sitting on the foot of Agnes' bed, looking from one child to another. They weren't bad little'uns. Spoiled, hurt and ignored perhaps, but not bad. Could they handle what she could tell of the real world, of her world?

"When I was a little girl and scared of monsters under the bed, and demons in the darkness, my mother would say to me; 'sing a gentle song, close your eyes up tight and wear a smile'." Sally smiled, thinking back to a much simpler time, many years ago, "It always worked. The monsters never got me. Until I met a real monster. This monster had no horns, or hoofs, or fangs. It was a man."

42

"Old Ron?" Agnes wrapped her arms around herself for comfort.

Nodding, Sally continued, "Now, no matter how tightly I screw up my eyes, no matter how sweet the song I sing or how much I try to smile... All I can see at night is his leering face coming upon me."

Standing, she smoothed down her dress, "You really should be sleeping."

Thomas shook his head, "I'll have bad dreams. I just know it."

"Sally?" Agnes' eyes were wide and wet. Were those tears? "What song did you sing to keep the monsters away? Could you... would you sing it for us now? Please?"

After a moment of silent indecision Sally smiled a little smile, closed her eyes, and sang a song she hadn't sung for a very long time.

Mr and Mrs Gutter paused mid-argument as the lilting sound of Sally's voice caressed their senses. It drifted like perfume through the house, briefly sweetening that sour place.

The Gutters slept soundly that night, but the still and peace of the night was broken by Sally's bad dreams, and the following morning by the renewed verbal fisticuffs between Mr and Mrs Gutter.

Over breakfast, Thomas and Agnes had regaled their mother with peculiar stories of their day in the park, and the terrifying old man who had crossed their path. Mrs Gutter was incensed by her offspring being subjected to the terrors of the criminal class, and the nefarious mischiefs they could be up to.

She berated her husband for employing a Nanny who would dare to bring unsavoury folk near her children. In turn, Mr Gutter raged against his judgement being questioned, and raised his hand to strike at his wife.

"You are trying my patience, woman!" He roared.

Mrs Gutter flung herself away from her husband before he could lay his fat hand upon her.

More red faced than normal, Mr Gutter slammed the front door as he exited the house on his way to work. The pictures hung in the hall were knocked askew by the force of the door connecting with the frame.

Hitting at the closed door Mrs Gutter hollered,

"I hate him I hate him I hate him! Why can't he be struck down in the street by a carriage!"

The Maid now made her entrance upon the scene, taking hold of Mrs Gutter's shaking shoulders and leading her away into the drawing room, with the promise of a cup of hot cocoa to calm her nerves.

Knock   Knock   Knock

Mrs Gutter looked over her shoulder in alarm at the tapping upon the knocker.

As soon as there was even a crack of an opening, Old Ron had slipped into the hall past the Maid and glided awkwardly across towards Mrs Gutter.

"Vagabond! Ruffian! Ragamuffin! Intruder!" The Maid cried out, clutching her hands to her breast in alarm.

Old Ron hissed at her, "Shut your big pudding muncher, you whelping whatsit! I'm here for Sally."

Finding a well of strength deep within which has not been spent by the mornings arguments, Mrs Gutter stood tall and rigid before the crooked man.

"Explain yourself, sir!" She stamped her foot, and Old Ron became still.

He attempted to recompose his features to be less alarming and less of an attack upon the senses. He unclenched his fists, and relaxed his arms and back. He bowed low, his long nose grazing the carpeted floor.

"Mrs Gutter I presume?" He grovelled.

"You know me?"

"You took me on two months back to clean your chimneys. A mighty fine job I did of it too, if I do say so my own self."

"That's about when the silver went missing." The Maid chimed in.

"Funny that, ain't it?" Ron shot the young woman a deadly glare with his small eyes, "I am here on an urgent errand. I must speak with Miss Rattles at once."

Mrs Gutter folded her arms, and Ron immediately knew he had used a poor choice of words.

"You *must*? You do not insist upon me in my own home! Sally is busy with the children at present, and I can see not how associating with the likes of you can do them or her any good at all."

Ron changed mental gears, and the well maintained machine of his snake-oil brain slipped into a more appropriate setting for this exchange. He bowed low once again.

45

"I apologise, dear lady." His south London twang left his voice fraction by fraction, until it more accurately mimicked that which Lady Gutter may find more favourable, "It was not my intention to put your nose out of joint by my uncomely manner. As you can see of me, I'm not a well-bred and fine gentleman like your mister must be."

He dared a quick glance up at her. It was working, she was softening to this grovelling approach, and so he upped his game once more.

"I prostrate myself before you and beg forgiveness. A pretty face as yours shouldn't be creased so; with worry."

Mrs Gutter failed to find a suitable reply, and instead flapped her jaw and muttered for a moment.

It is in this quiet pause that Sally, flanked by Thomas and Agnes descended the grand stairs and became aware of the presence of Old Ron in the house. Thomas and Agnes instinctively moved to hide behind Sally.

Mrs Gutter regained some of her composure following the uncommon experience of flattery and flirtation, "Ah, Sally, here you are. This gentleman has come calling for you."

Old Ron took centre stage before Sally or the children could reply or offer a retort to the phrase 'gentleman' in relation to the old criminal.

"You see, dear lady, an old friend of Sally's and mine is knocking on death's door. A terrible tragedy has beset our family of friends. He'll soon be a-tapping on them pearly gates for a seat in the eternal fluffy here-after. He has requested Sally by his side when he goes."

The Maid made protest of Sally departing for the day, aghast at the potential of having the children abandoned to her care, "I'm too busy for all that malarkey."

Sally cautiously took in Ron's body language, and where he may be concealing a knife about his person today.

"Uncle Woo is not long for this world."

Mrs Gutter swept to her Nanny, emotional and overcome, "Sally, go to your friend. You simply must. Take the children."

"Wait, what?" Sally blurted, "Take them to see a dying man?"

Mrs Gutter could not be persuaded. She did not care what the children did or saw, so long as they were out of her hair and not under her feet. To her, they were little more than a noisy and expensive inconvenience.

"I shan't hear another word about it!"

Mrs Gutter was so keen for the house to be empty, and to be quiet that she nearly pushed them all, Maid included out of the front door, there were tears welling in her eyes.

"Good day to you, beautiful Lady." Old Ron doffed a hat he wasn't wearing, and offered Mrs Gutter his handkerchief.

She looked at it, pulling back from the stained and mucky item.

"It's dirty." Said she.

"No, Lady. It's honest. It, nor I, hide ourselves behind finery and good manners, when there is no call for them."

47

He dropped the handkerchief on the floor before slipping sideways out of the slowly closing front door.

Old Ron led them a disorientating zigzag through the city's back streets. Even under bright morning light many of these places were dark and dangerous. As they moved into areas containing factories and warehouses, Ron began to talk loudly, not to Sally or to anyone else present, but to the world around him.

"Lime House district. Dark alleys. Deep, still canals. Empty warehouses. Open sewers. Wary eyes peeping out at you from the shadows. The sound of underhanded goings on emanating from every nook and cranny."

Sally kept the children pulled in close. Ron didn't ever let them out of his sight, and she worried that though she might be able to run away and reach safety, Thomas would likely be the slower of the three of them, and the first to be caught, and... Sally didn't like to think of what Ron might do in that scenario. Best to play along with the mad old coot until a better plan came to mind.

"Dark things grin in the shadows of night. Dark things dream of taking that first bite! Dark things dwell in arches, under bridges, over doors. Dark things snigger with their rat-a-tat jaws!"

Agnes suspected the old man had lost his mind, and she wasn't too far from the truth.

Through thickening London smog and hazy sunlight the hunched and creaking man led them to a deep and foreboding set of buildings, tightly packed along a thin,

48

winding street. At a low door he stopped, and beckoned for Sally and the children to go inside.

After a moment's hesitation, they did.

The rooms beyond the small front door were dimly lit with red lamps and lanterns decorated in the style of the far-east. Men lay about upon cushions and fabric, bleary eyed and sweaty. Gentlemen and ruffians, equally floored by the Dragon, whose lair they had entered.

"What's that smell?" Agnes asked, screwing up her nose.

"Opium." Sally replied grimly, "Try not to breathe in too deeply."

Thomas and Agnes held hands.

Ron showed them through a beaded curtain at the back of the maze of rooms. This space was better illuminated, sparsely furnished, and covered in blood.

Uncle Woo, a small Chinese man lay slumped in the corner of the room.

The children gasped and Sally turned, hugging their faces to her to hide their view.

Ron began to laugh.

"You killed him?" Sally was aghast.

Ron nudged the prone man with a foot. He stirred slightly, struggling to lift his head.

"Sally?"

The delicate man had a thin white moustache, now stained red with blood and spit from his mouth.

Ron chuckled, "Did you think I wouldn't find out where you'd gone?"

So this was a punishment.

Uncle Woo had helped Sally escape from Old Ron, and aided her in starting a new life. For an Opium fiend, he was gentle, kind and a fatherly presence the like of which Sally had never known. Now he sat creased in a corner, Ron's dagger having traced deep crimson lines across his chest and arms and stomach.

"I'm so sorry." Sally was welling up, anger and a hot hot fear mixing and curdling in her gut.

Woo nodded, a small smile pricking up the sides of his moustache. Then he died. His head lolled forward, and the breath in his lungs escaped in a slow wheeze.

Old Ron laughed.

"Fine. This is my punishment. I get it. Now we're going." Sally began to push the children out through the beaded curtain, but Ron took hold of her wrist and stopped her exit.

He pointed to a wooden box in the corner. It was inlaid with a pattern of crossing lines and squares, and possessed no obvious hinges or clasps or handles by which it could be opened. Uncle Woo's puzzle box.

"So now not only is this a murder, it's a robbery too?" Sally felt sick.

The smell of blood was invading her nose. She feared she may never be rid of it.

Ron pulled Sally back into the room, and nodded to the box. He was giggling still, unable to control himself, the Opium thick in the air was addling his power of speech.

"Only you know how to open the damnable contraption. He only bestowed that secret upon your fine self." He managed, through deep pauses for breath between guffaws and giggles and chuckles.

"Because what's inside that box is mine." Sally did not move to open it.

"You're a horrid beast!" Agnes coughed up phlegm and spat at Old Ron.

Sally, impressed by the girl's aim though she was, shouted for her to stay back and to keep schtum.

Ron didn't stop laughing, not even pausing to wipe the gob from his cloak. Picking up the box, he shook it, listening for a jingle of jewels or the chink of coins.

"Woo's treasure box. The man was wealthy as a king!" Ron's little eyes didn't leave Sally, they held her still, penetrating her.

"Outside. Can we please get outside. I'll show you how to open it once we're out of here."

She indicated the body of Uncle Woo, and reluctantly Ron nodded. Still giggling and chortling, he pushed his three prisoners ahead of him and out of the Opium den.

The smog of the street was a welcome relief to the close atmosphere of the subterranean lair of the Dragon. Sally took deep lungfuls of London air, wiping her brow. Thomas and Agnes huddled close to her, yet just out of reach. They were both scared, and though Agnes was putting on a good show of bravery for her younger brother, it was clear that she could break at any moment.

Ron threw to Sally the puzzle box. She caught it clumsily, and gently rested it on the ground.

Now that they were away from the invasive influence of the Opium smoke, Ron's laughter began to subside. His knife reappeared. Still it wore a red gown of blood, not yet wiped clean since its use upon poor Uncle Woo.

Sally knelt down beside the box, and felt along it's surfaces. Her fingers worked swiftly, sliding one edge of the box away from the others at an angle, then pulling at another. The box was then a rectangle and not a cube, and she pressed her fingers into minute depressions on the top, amidst the lattice of delicate inlay. The box clicked, and the concealed lid popped open slightly.

Hungry for whatever treasure may lay inside, Old Ron hurried forward, his eyes gleaming. He pulled from the box a handful of items, none of which were the treasure he was expecting. There was a small blanket, a necklace, and a photograph.

"What is *this*?" The old man hissed, coiling like a serpent in a subdued rage, "Where is the *loot*?"

Sally reached forward gently and took the items from him.

"Woo was smart unlike you, dickhead. He never kept his money here. He sent it all home to his family in China."

Ron's bottom jaw quivered angrily, "Then what is *this*?"

Sally held up the photograph for Ron to see. He flew into a sudden rage, lunging at Sally with his knife. She was ready for it, and the two of them struggled on the floor. The blade flew close to both their faces as they rolled across the ground. Agnes and Thomas rushed forward, trying to pull their Nanny free of Ron's vicious coils.

"Fucking run!" Sally called to them, "Get away! Find a Copper! Get yourselves safe!"

"We can't leave you!" Agnes protested, grabbing hold of the hem of Ron's cloak and pulling it taught.

It pinched at the man's thin neck and his attention turned briefly away from his prey. Sally took the opportunity to punch him square in the jaw. He fell back from her as she scrambled upright, panting.

"Get *away*!" Sally screamed at the children.

The shock of her cry rendered Agnes and Thomas immobile for a moment.

Ron once more taking hold of Sally and the recommencement of their struggle triggered an explosion of speed from both of the young Gutters. They fled, hand in hand, as fast as their little feet could carry them.

Some time later, a bloodied and shaking hand retrieved the items once held by Woo's puzzle box from the ground. They were held tight, and tears were shed.

PART TWO

Old Ron's words echoed in her head.

"What did I tell you, my little wall flower? I own you. Everything you are and is was forged by the hot fires of my bitter lust and hard mastery. Without me you wouldn't exist, you'd still be that nameless girl, earning pennies per ride at Flinching's Whore House! Without me there is no you! I am your world, I am your moon, I am your sun!"

The household at 17 Spindle Street shook to the impact of warheads and the detonation of landmines fired and laid down by Mr and Mrs Gutter. What had come before were mere skirmishes compared to the brutality of today's conflict. War between the pair was always simmering, occasionally boiling over, but never really, truly, absolutely catching light.

Vases smashed upon the floor, a chair was blown to shrapnel, and pictures fell from the walls under the bombardment. There was no shelter from this onslaught.

Agnes and Thomas had told their parents of their visit to the Opium den of Uncle Woo at the behest of the loathsome Old Ron. They had listened, mouths agape as the tale unravelled before them. Not once did they offer their offspring comfort, or a cuddle, or a simple caring word. Mr Gutter blamed Mrs for sending them off with the man when he called. Mrs Gutter blamed Mr for employing Sally in the first place. Back and forth with blame they jousted, as Agnes and Thomas stood and watched, tears in their eyes and dirt on their clothes.

Mr Gutter moved like a landslide, pounding around the room, his great guts swinging like a battering ram at anything that dared to get in his way; furniture or family. Mrs Gutter strained herself tighter and pulled herself more taught, so much so that she might snap in half. Veins stood out on her forehead and neck, and her arms rigid at her side were vibrating with potential energy. She was an elastic band, stretched until it could stretch no more. She snapped.

"I want a divorce!"

Mrs Gutter screamed the words into her husband's blustering face. For the first time in a very long time he heard what she said, and listened. He could not believe it, and told her so.

"I will have none of your insufferable Suffragette silliness in this house." Said he.

Mrs Gutter, now free of her buildup of tension, sagged limply into a chair, resting her head in her hands, unable to look up at her Husband or children.

Agnes and Thomas were rooted to where they stood. They remained there unsure whether to run, to hide, or to add something to the argument.

Unheard by the Gutters, the door had been knocked upon and answered. Sally Rattles, one arm over the Maid's shoulders for support, entered the scene.

Mr Gutter's attention rounded on her like a searchlight, glaring, bright and intrusive.

"Explain yourself! The children have told us everything! About you. About what you've been getting up to with that Ron character. The whole bally lot! I've a mind to summon the constabulary!"

"Yet you haven't." Sally winked at the young Gutterlings, a reassurance that all will be well, "Might be a scandal, eh? Wouldn't want that, would you?"

Agnes noticed Sally wince, and the stains of blood on her clothes. She moved to say something, but Sally made a small shake of her head that said 'don't you worry about silly old Sally'.

"I came back to check on the children. Make sure they got back in one piece… before I go."

"Go?" Thomas was startled and shocked by the prospect of her leaving.

"Best just to slip away, to not cause you any more problems."

Mrs Gutter rose from her chair and walked slowly towards Sally. She seemed to have a new composure and a new clarity behind her eyes.

"Despite all that we have been told about you, you came back?" Said she, "Knowing they'd have told us of the whole vile affair, you came back for them?"

Sally nodded. Facing the consequences of her actions is something she had always shied away from, and avoided at all costs. But not any longer. Too much had happened to these children in too short a space of time to just up and leave with no word of goodbye, and no apology. "Have you ever killed a man, Mr Gutter?" Sally asked of the mountainous man.

56

He was quite taken aback by the inquiry, "What? Of course not! Have you?"

"No. Almost did though, I think."

The adult Gutters began to regard Sally in a very new light. Not only had the uncouth woman fought to save her own life, she fought to save the lives of her charges as well. No Nanny had ever gone so far for them. No Nanny had ever needed to until today, but that was by the by.

"I think it best you go at once. Children, go and clean yourselves up, you look a disgrace." Mr Gutter's voice was low, but rising to its usual strength and volume as he reasserted control upon the household.

Agnes and Thomas didn't wait to be told twice.

"You're right, of course." He admitted, "We do *not* want a scandal. What would the neighbours think?"

Mrs Gutter was exasperated, she waved her arms around as she spoke, yet did not reach the shrieking heights of any of her previous forays into fury.

"To Hell with the neighbours, to hell with hiding from scandal, and to hell with you!"

Mr Gutter was not sure how to deal with this new, more composed version of his wife. It tripped him up; in what was a familiar mental game of cat and mouse, there was now suddenly no mouse, there was something else.

"For pities sake, woman. The children need stability in their lives. They need to be taught the right path."

"You mean *your* path."

Mr Gutter began to wax lyrical on the good honest day's work a man can do in a fine, stable, secure job at a very fine, stable, secure British bank. He insisted upon how it builds fortitude of character, sturdiness of mind and strength in the backbone.

"Sounds like a riot." Sally muttered sarcastically, loud enough only for the Maid and children to hear.

Louder, and wincing, she addressed the parent Gutters, "So that's settled then. Tomorrow the children will accompany you for a day at the bank."

Mr Gutter floundered, suddenly wrong-footed yet again.

"A day's honest work assisting their father, to see how they can be fortified in character, sturdier in mind and stronger in the backbone." Sally nodded with a sense of finality.

The Maid, cooing at Sally to look after herself, led the injured woman from the room and up the stairs. Sally tried to protest, that she must go, that she cannot and should not stay. As they mounted the wide stairs, the Maid leaned in conspiratorially.

"They'll never forgive me for saying, but a bit of rough love is what this family needs; shaking them out of their rut. You're doing nothing but good for them, mark my words. It'll be right in the end."

The Maid coaxed Sally up the stairs and to her small room, where she was undressed, bandaged and put to bed.

"Rest now. You might act tough as old boots, but you'll still bleed and die like the rest of us."

"I shall not leave this topic alone." Mrs Gutter was tapping her foot.

"What topic?"

Mr Gutter sank into an armchair and it strained under his weight. His face was pale and he found himself slave to an unsettling and unusual feeling; that of uncertainty.

"I want a divorce." Mrs Gutter repeated her earlier statement, but calmly, with a cool head, and a steady nerve, "It've driving me to the mad house, living here with you."

Mr Gutter shook his head,
"No. No divorce. I shall not be seen as a failure."

Mrs Gutter's brow creased, struck by her husband's uncommonly frank retort.

"A failure?" Said she, snorting, "Failing is what you do best."

Agnes and Thomas crept up the servant's staircase and to the door to Sally's room. Agnes raised her hand to knock, but it was pulled open from within.

"I heard you coming." Sally said, clutching her side, "Herd of elephants, you two."

She moved back and allowed the children into her room, just the uncomfortable side of snug, now that three bodies occupied it. Both children hugged her tightly, and she stroked their hair.

"Now now," She softly sighed, "Don't go wiping your snotty noses on my nightie."

Thomas giggled, and relaxed. Agnes still clung tightly. Prising herself slowly free of their vice-like embraces, she cosied herself into bed, and the children joined her there. It was a tight fit for all three of them. Agnes sat up at the foot end, and Thomas curled up between them.

"I think I owe you both an apology. Or an explanation. Or something of the like."

The young Gutters weren't sure what to say, or even if anything needed to be said and so they remained mute, affectionately ensconced with Sally in her narrow bed.

Sally began to tell Agnes and Thomas a story. It was a tale she hadn't recounted aloud before, and it was fragmentary, and some bits didn't make too much sense, but they began to understand Sally that much more, and why she came back, and why she cared.

"My mother sells breadcrumbs," She began, "To feed a flock of birds. Replacements for the children she abandoned."

Sally's childhood had been spent as an unwanted obstacle in her mother's life, as had several sisters and brothers before her. She wasn't sure how many, and she didn't know their names. She didn't even know her own.

When no longer a child, but not yet a woman, she was sold to a house of carnal pleasures. Madame Flinching exploited her charges, barely feeding or caring for them, aside from the occasional inspection for unwanted pregnancies. Other girls there would vanish briefly from time to time, and when they came back were ashen and broken, shadows of their former selves.

Finally Sally was given a name. She was gifted it by a man named Ron, who she thought for so long had broken her out of Madame Flinching's whore house. The truth of it was that he had purchased her, and for not a very great sum. He controlled all that she did. He made her believe that they were the victims of a great conspiracy, that she must remain hidden and obedient, for fear of giving them away. They addled their thoughts with gin and opium, and mind altering treats bought from travelling salesmen and dirty back-alley allotments. They were always on the move, staying with friends and acquaintances and contacts and consorts across the city.

But Sally discovered the truth. A night spent hiding at Uncle Woo's loosened Ron's tongue and in a stupor he told her the truth. He owned her.

"The only reason I bought you," He had said, "Was to keep other men's paws off of you. I wanted you all to myself. You're *my* play thing."

The kindly Chinese man assisted in her plot to escape his clutches, and hid her for several months. He hid her for nine months. She was with child.

Ron's baby never cried, or laughed, or opened its eyes. It was born cold and pale.

Uncle Woo promised to keep Sally's secret, and stored some items of Sally's safely in his puzzle box when she went out and tried to make a life for herself on her own. Within the puzzle box Sally placed a necklace she had purchased for the baby, its blanket, and a photograph of her holding the infant. Despite the vile man whose progeny it was, she loved it with all her aching heart.

She tried finding work, but could not. Everywhere she went the shadow of Old Ron was found lurking. Quite desperate and alone she returned to drinking, and one misty morning, slowly recovering from the night before, was when she stumbled upon a queue of old women waiting at the door of 17 Spindle Street.

"And you know the rest, as you were there."

"Put these pennies in your pockets."

Mr Gutter instructed his children as they left the house early the next day. Agnes and Thomas had remained obstinate and downcast, despite his best efforts to chivvy them up and to cheer them for what lay ahead.

To the young Gutters working at the bank sounded like a terribly dreary way to waste your life. They each took the offered coins from their father, one each, and tucked them away safely. They trailed in his wake as he marched them along the wide pavements and tree-lined roads near their home. As they travelled, Mr Gutter once again attempted to encourage his children and enthuse them for the long hours they would spend in his company.

"Today is about structure! Today is about discipline! Two things about which I doubt the feisty miss Rattles knows a great deal."

"I'd feel safer if she was with us." Thomas said quietly to his sister, who nodded.

Every shaded street corner or sudden movement in a crowd was made into the form of Old Ron by their troubled imaginations. He would be a bush, or a lamp post, or hiding between two bickering biddies.

They reached a large open square, flanked on three sides by imposing neoclassical buildings; all thick columns and dramatically posed statues of fallen heroes of yore. The largest of these buildings was The Bank. It didn't need another name. It was the first, the oldest, the richest and the stuffiest of them all.

In the middle of the square a flock of pigeons bounced about, fluttering in small waves into the air and back to earth again, orbiting a small lady sat cross legged amidst them. She held close to her a basket of small paper bags.

"Feed the birds, guv'nor?" She offered a parcel of breadcrumbs to Mr Gutter as he passed, "Only a penny for a bag."

Mr Gutter held his nose in the air and refused to acknowledge her existence.

Thomas pulled on Agnes' sleeve. It's her! It's Sally's mother!

"I want to feed the birds." Said he, stopping to watch the curious pigeons peck at the ground and hop about on their little orange toes.

Mr Gutter rounded on his children, his cheeks reddening, "Do not look to make a show of yourselves, not today."

"She looks half starved." Agnes murmured.

His volcanic glare bore down on his offspring, and they reluctantly followed his lead, moving away from the woman and her flock.

"There's no use in giving her money to feed those pests. She has enough food for herself, only she's making the mistake of filling the bellies of those pigeons rather than her own."

      Inside the bank was colder by several degrees than the weather outside. Marble and iron and gilt sapped any warmth and stole it away. As the Gutters make their way through the atrium, they found themselves circled by the bird-like faces of The Bank's managerial department. They each had hooked noses and a strange stooped posture, which reminded Agnes of the great carnivorous birds she had seen in zoos.

      "And what, prey tell, are these?" Asked the more nimble of the three Managers.

      Mr Gutter introduced his children, and in turn introduced them to the frightful Messrs Calvus, Gyps and Barbatus. They each seemed to loom over the children, cold and unfeeling, but hungry.

      "The man thinks a bank is an appropriate place to bring his offspring?" Mr Gyps cawed, shocked and amused by the apparent absurdity of the thought.

      Mr Gutter pulled at his collar to loosen it a fraction. His red face was redder still, now confronted by the very tip top of the management tree, and the predators that lurked there. He explained there had been some discipline issues at home, and that he was endeavouring to demonstrate to his younglings how a solid, honest, humble day's work would set them upon the straight and narrow path to success.

"A vaguely plausible notion." Mr Barbatus shrugged, "though not, I fear, one that you came upon willingly?"

Mr Gutter ploughed on, not wanting to appear fainthearted before either his children or his superiors, "...to show them structure, the joys of conformity and the heaven of a well-balanced ledger."

"This is not a school yard." Mr Gyps snapped his bill at the large man, unintimidated by the vast size difference between the two of them.

Mr Calvus was stroking his chin thoughtfully, "The heaven of a well-balanced ledger?" He repeated Mr Gutter's words.

"Thomas wanted to spend his penny frivolously, on a bag of breadcrumbs to feed to the pigeons."

"A penny wasted!"

Crowing and mewling, the three men circled the children, berating them for such an irresponsible use of money.

"But instead we are here, ready to set it into an investment account, and to watch it flourish."

Thomas clutched the penny in his pocket, and Agnes rested her hands on his shoulders protectively.

"I want to feed the birds." He insisted.

Stupidity! Short-sightedness! Idiocy! The Managers squawked and beat their arms like wings.

"Invest! Invest! Invest!"

Mr Calvus advances on Thomas, his hands outstretched like talons.

"Give me your penny, boy."

Thomas doesn't hesitate to move. If the events of recent days had taught him anything; it is to run away as quickly as you can and find safety if you feel you must.

He launched himself bodily at the approaching man, knocking into him with his whole diminutive weight. The old man was bowled over by the impact, and the boy leaped over him and raced for the large doors of The Bank.

Agnes called after her brother, snared by her father's meaty fist upon her wrist. She could not give chase.

"Get back here this instant!" he bellowed after his son's rapidly retreating form.

"Let go of me! I hate you!" Agnes dug her nails into her father's hand in a bid for freedom, but his grip only tightened.

Mr Gyps and Mr Barbatus were lifting their stricken fellow to his spatted feet, all three of them bore expressions of doom and rage.

Agnes bit her father on the back of his hand. Her teeth sunk deeply into his skin. Instinctively he released her hand, but swung at her with his other. It caught her across the side of her head and sent her spinning across the floor, landing face first on hard marble.

The hushed onlookers within the bank gasped, and an eyrie silence fell across the scene. Thomas' rapid footsteps faded and he was gone.

Mr Gutter looked around him, searching out some way to regain some control of the situation. The room shrank in upon him, walls of eyes and judging frowns.

Hobbling towards the gargantuan form quivering before him, Mr Calvus spoke loudly so that everyone might hear him.

"They say one mellows with age, Gutter. Who *they* are I can not fathom, but it is complete tommyrot. You are a disgrace! An inept banker, a feckless father and a total waste of space!"

"But sir..."

"Get out, Gutter. You no longer work here."

The three men nodded in unison, turned on their clawed heels and stalked away. At the edges of the room muttered conversations began to float in his direction. He didn't need to know what they were saying. He could guess. He flushed a deep crimson in embarrassment, and began to hurry from The Bank.

"Excuse me," Snapped a woman as he reached the door, "I think you're forgetting something."

She pointed to Agnes, only now beginning to pull herself from her prone position upon the floor.

Thomas ran and ran and ran, his eyes bleary with tears and sobs wracking his small chest. He didn't stop or look back, he didn't want to. He had run away before, but only briefly to antagonise their horrible Nannies. Now he was running away, and he meant for it to be forever.

Left and right, over bridges and under overhanging buildings he wove a twisting, turning path through the city. He rebounded off of the wide skirts of fashionable ladies, tripped over the walking canes of elegant gentlemen, and cried out when he suddenly came upon the Thames and almost fell straight in.

Lucky for him a small houseboat had been moored below, and he fell on his back onto a relatively forgiving canvas hold covering. Smack!

It was not as soft as it looked. He groaned and cried and lay staring at the muggy grey sky, sea birds and pigeons circling and spiralling overhead.

A bearded face poked up from the cabin of the houseboat.

"What's wrong with you boy?" It asked.

Thomas' sobs were choked back, and he sat up. "Everything."

The bearded face raised an eyebrow, "That so?"

Thomas nodded, "I'm going to live on the street and be a vagabond. A ragamuffin."

"Trust me boy that's the worst thing in the world you could do."

With some small amount of bribery, the bearded houseboat owner persuaded Thomas to come down from the canvas, and to be taken home. Hot cocoa and biscuits filling his tummy, Thomas felt less sad and afraid. He still feared reprisals from his parents upon his return, but the thought of finding comfort with Agnes and Sally was a happy counterpoint to that trepidation.

"They'll be glad to see you safe and sound, I'll wager. They must be worried sick."

***

"Down on your luck, mister?" Old Ron loomed from the darkness of an alley, slithering to perch his crooked frame on a low wall overlooking the river.

Mr Gutter slumped amongst the debris at the back of the shops behind which he had hidden himself. Empty crates and broken boxes and the stink of waste and the dank atmosphere of the Thames swallowed him up. He leaned back on a stack of old newspapers, staring up at the same sky as his son, some few hundred yards further downriver.

The large man didn't respond, but that did not bother Ron one bit.

"Just trying to be a friend. Looks like you might need one."

He picked up Mr Gutter's discarded bowler hat, casually flicking it free of dirt.

"Everyone needs friends, sir." His small pale eyes took in every small nuanced movement of the large man's face, and what may be trickling through his brain.

"A whole spectrum of people is required in life. Friends, those who come and go with little consequence, lovers... enemies."

He brushed a hand across his own face, tracing a finger down a recently acquired wound which might one day provide him with quite a fantastic scar.

Mr Gutter riled slightly, "Lovers? The only woman I ever loved hates me."

Old Ron put on his pitiful condolences face, which encouraged Mr Gutter to open up a little more.

"I provided her with a fine house and money to buy herself pretty things."

Old Ron shook his head slowly, now slipping into his persona of mysterious wise old man.

"I've known a few women in my time, and pretty things have only kept their view of me rosy for a time. They need... looking after... If you don't treat them right they leave."

Mr Gutter nodded.

"That's their power over men. They can choose when it's over. They become cold and hard, and flee in the dead of night."

Old Ron watched his victim intently, his eyes unblinking, drawing the man into his words as would a hypnotist.

"The only way to *truly* maintain control, to maintain a lasting power over them, their thoughts, their actions..."

Mr Gutter slowly leaned forward, curious as to what secret wisdom might be bestowed upon him.

"...is to leave them first."

This did not seem to Mr Gutter like the miraculous solution Ron had built it up to be. He shook his head and pulled himself from his throne of detritus. He advanced on Old Ron, holding out a hand for his hat, which the wizened old creature offered up with a cheerful smile. The two of them paused there, at the low wall, looking in opposite directions. Mr Gutter took in the foul smell of the Thames, and the dusty grey view of the city on the opposite bank. Old Ron looked at the mountains of rotting rubbish and discarded and broken shop equipment.

"Seems to me you're at the end of your tether." Ron said, leaning ever so slightly towards the other man.

And he was right. Mr Gutter craved control, and order, and success and obedience. Yet all of these things evaded him in his life, which was now nought but a chaotic helter-skelter ride into the cesspool of humiliation. He looked over the low wall and to the muddy brown water sloshing up and down below him. The wall was low on this side but steep and tall on the other. The water was several feet below, the spray of it hitting the wall moistened his face. He felt like a rope in a tug of war. One by one his little threads had worn thin, frayed and tattered.

Old Ron asked the large man what he would say to his wife, if she would only listen. What would he say to his wife, from the bottom of his heart?

Taking a slow, deep breath Mr Gutter thought about what he would say, closing his eyes, picturing the scene before he spoke. As he opened his mouth to utter the first word a mighty blow to the back of his head sent him forward over the wall. Splosh!

He hit the water hard, mouth open. His lungs filled with the turgid foul water as he gasped for air, flailing his bloated arms and legs uselessly.

Old Ron watched the large man disappear beneath the surface. Clapping his hands together in satisfaction, he smiled, then vanished into the shadows of the nearby back streets.

***

Agnes had been taken home by a teller from The Bank, and charged Mrs Gutter the fee for the transport. Now the girl sat swaddled in several blankets next to her brother on their mother's chaise lounge, flanked by the women of the house. Mrs Gutter found herself to be incredulous, and did not wish to believe that her husband had been let go from his position. The Maid, stunned but unsurprised by the man's actions applied a cold compress to the girl's injured head, where a bruise the colour and texture of a plum was beginning to show. Sally stalked the room, her countenance hard and unreadable. Now and again she flinched, holding her side where she was bandaged while using her umbrella as a support.

The Children clung to each other beneath the blankets, cold and struggling with emotions they couldn't name or understand.

With a crack and a crash the back door of 17 Spindle Street was broken open, and a parade of savage dusty men rushed inside. Following them, using his old widely bristled chimney brush as a staff, Old Ron made his entrance.

The sweeps made swift work of locating the women and children, holding them hostage in their own home. Dirty shoes left sooty prints on every carpet. Grimy hands left greasy trails on all that they touched.

Mrs Gutter stood in the centre of the room, turning a cold and daring look slowly upon each of the soot-blackened men. Finally she settled her glare upon Old Ron.

"What do you want?" She asked simply.

He nodded to Sally, not in response, but by way of invitation to speak.

"Revenge." Said she.

Mrs Gutter rankled at the savage man, but he shouted over her words.

"That's no way for a widow to be carrying on."

Frozen by his words, Mrs Gutter's mind leaped somersaults and the bottom dropped out of her guts. She fell back, nearly missing a chair. The Maid rushed to her side. Old Ron laughed and the chimney sweeps jeered as the tale of Mr Gutter's fall was recounted.

Sally shook in shock and in anger. She should never have come to this house. All she had brought them was a misery worse than the one in which they had already been wallowing. She began this frightful chain of events, and so somehow she must be the one to end them.

"Leave them alone. I'll come back with you. Willingly."

Old Ron looked Sally up and down, his mouth hanging loosely open, eager, but cautious.

"It's a bit late for that now, Sal." Said he, "I promised the lads a bit of sport. Got them all riled up and keen. Shame to disappoint them."

He held his arms out to his blackened cohorts. With a wave of his bent hands he set them loose. They roared and laughed and charged about the room, hungry and with rigid pricks. Beasts in body and in deed, they tore at the clothes of the Maid and Mrs Gutter, threw Thomas from the room and dragged Agnes into a cupboard. Sally beat at the men with her umbrella as best she was able

73

through the pain in her side, screaming out for them to stop! Leave them alone! They have done nothing wrong!

Old Ron had given them instructions to leave Sally to him, but a couple of the men chose to follow their own instincts rather than instructions, and she found herself buried beneath their savage lustful hands. Ron's dagger jabbed at their backs, and they folded back from her, yelping.

"Ron, please, no!"

Sally once again began to pull at the men atop Mrs Gutter and the Maid, her umbrella in her hand as a baton, raining down on the men's backs.

Grabbing her and dragging her from the room, Old Ron confided in the terrified and desperate woman who knelt before him.

"You were my favourite toy." He sneered as he raised his dagger.

His eyes bulged wide and his mouth hung loosely open, gasping suddenly. He dropped the dagger and ran his hands over his body. Sally had rammed the pointed end of her umbrella into his chest, where she knew a wound already lay.

The black fabric article pierced him through the chest, protruding slightly from his back.

Sally backed away from her former lover and owner, startled by her own actions. One of the ravenous men noticed the fall of their leader. Blood pumped through Ron's clothes, pooling upon the floor around his prone body. Sally advanced slowly to check if he was dead. She took hold of the umbrella and wiggled it. He did not react.

74

The men, moving away from Mrs Gutter and the Maid now, subdued by the death of Old Ron, rounded on Sally.

She pulled the makeshift weapon from his torso, and used it as a means to stand once again. She leant on it heavily, now bent and ripped from its insertion into a man's rib cage.

"What are you fuckers looking at?" She spat at them, "You want to try your luck? Try it with me!"

She brandished the umbrella like a sword.

Deflated and leaderless the men did not have the inclination to continue. They backed away from the crazed woman flicking blood across the walls as she waved the umbrella too and fro.

The men departed, each heading off in a different direction once out of the house, melting into shadows and vanishing around corners.

"I've called the police." Thomas said, his voice shaking, from the foot of the stairs.

Once he had heard the women scream, and the thundering roar of the men he had raced to the telephone and frantically called for the constabulary.

"Well done." Sally smiled at him.

She covered Mrs Gutter and the Maid with blankets, retrieved Agnes from the cupboard and gave her instructions on how to care for the women, and what to say to the police once they arrived.

"What are you going to do?" The girl asked testily, as she began to fuss about her mother in a most adult and practical way.

Sally did not reply. She hobbled from the room, and down the stairs, and across the hall, and out of the front door of 17 Spindle Street.

Sirens could be heard approaching from her right, so she turned left and hurried away as best she was able with a broken umbrella for a walking stick.

She blew in on a westerly wind, clutching her tattered and broken umbrella like her life depended on it. Slumping amongst the crates and boxes at the docks, she hoped to go unnoticed by the workers, loading ships bound for exotic and colourful lands far overseas. She wondered if she might perhaps stow aboard, and find herself a new life in one of those colourful far flung places. Her bandage had come loose, and she could feel the warmth and wetness of blood soaking into her clothes. Looking at the crate by which she slumped, she found it to be marked 'rum', and thought to herself; *'don't mind if I do.'*

THE END

Straight On 'Til Mourning

Around the grave of Captain Hook dance the merry Lost Boys. A roughly hewn headstone marks the spot, erected by the Pirates for their fallen Captain, finally bested by the Eternal Boy; Peter Pan. Around and around the grave of Captain Hook dance and sing the merry Lost Boys.

"Tick-a tock goes the clock in the belly of the croc!"

"Snap-a clap-a goes the trap-a with a jaw of steel!"

"No man or maid or creature slain could save him from this end!"

"All that's left, a rusty hook, that bravely Mister Peter took!"

Peter lands lightly upon the headstone, sitting as if upon nothing more important than a stool.

"Oh, but we should give our fallen foe a moment of peaceful respect. Captain Codfish-"

The Lost Boys snigger and giggle.

"-a game well played, and lost."

Peter tosses the hook upon the freshly turned soil. The boys gasp, as the item that instilled such fear lays before them, beaten and corroded, discarded.

Peter shrugs, "I shan't need it."

Then, crowing like a cockerel, Peter hops into the air, Tinkerbell at his side, and away into the forest they fly. The Lost Boys holler and whoop and jump and sing their song once more. They skip and cheer and they too merge with the foliage around them, and are gone. Their cruel and jubilant song muffled by the giant leaves and mighty trunks of the trees of the forest of The Neverland.

78

Some great many years previously, a man of noble birth had fallen on hard times. He sailed the seas and oceans of the globe in search of riches and wealth. His wife believed him to be Captain of a great merchant vessel that sailed regularly to the New World of the Americas, and she cried many of the long lonely nights, wishing him safely back to her and their two young children.
Every night she would tell them a bed time story, tuck them into their beds of thin sheets, and put just one more small shovelful of coal on the fire to keep them warm as they drifted off to sleep.

"Goodnight Minnie. Goodnight Stanley. I love you both slightly more than yesterday." This she would say to them every night, as she left them to their dreams.

The rare nights on which her husband was home, the children would climb excitedly onto his lap, and he would regale them all with fantastical stories of far-flung lands, strange peoples and sea monsters. It is one such evening as this that begins the greatest and saddest adventure of this man's life, for unbeknownst to him, a Shadow listens at the window. Attached to this Shadow is a strange boy with hollow eyes. He listens to the stories, and imagines how wonderful it must be to sail the seas and see such amazing places. But there is nowhere so amazing as the place this boy calls home, yet he is lonely. He is always lonely.

Once the children have been tucked into their beds, and the husband and wife are dozing by the fire, into the room slips the Boy. His Shadow slides across the room, looking in draws and under chairs for any little trinket or treasure that catches its dark eyes. The Boy gently wakes the children, and as quietly as he can, he steals them away. But years at sea with a cut-throat crew have sharpened the wits of their father like a fine sword blade. He wakes, knowing that something is afoot and sees, agog, his children swept away into the sky. He calls out and snatches at them from the window, but he cannot reach them in time. It is not onto empty air that his hands close. No! He catches hold of the strange boy's Shadow, and tears it from him. It struggles, and silently screams to be set free, but the man holds it tight.

Overturning one of his children's toy chests, divesting it of it's gleeful contents, he pushes the struggling Shadow into it, and closes it tight, sealing it shut with the latch.

"What's happening?" Asks the Mother, rubbing her eyes of sleep, "Where are the children?"

"They are gone." Says the Father, staring at the toy chest and its silently struggling occupant.

The very next morning he kisses her goodbye, and makes swiftly to his ship, taking with him nothing but the toy chest, never to see her again. He does not explain to his crew where they are bound, for he does not know that himself.

"Where are we headed, Captain Hake?" Asks the Boatswain.

Clutching the toy chest, the Captain says, "We follow the Shadow."

And so they do.

They make a glass box into which they place the shadow. Every day it tries to flee, and take off to its owner. Every day it fails, and every day the confused crew follow the direction in which it stares, craving a reconnection to the Boy.

The course is a muddled zigzag, taking them to mysterious unknown islands shrouded in mist and cloud, to vast cities of paper castles, and further, further, further off of any known map. Each of their destinations is a welcome rest stop, but the Captain refuses to remain still for long. He seeks out mystics, hermits, cartographers, treasure hunters and other such people, all of them prove to know nothing of the strange Boy or his Shadow.

Once every blue moon does he discover a person who half-remembers a dream they had when a child; A dream of a far away land full of adventure and laughter, ruled over by a strange flying Boy. One grey day the Shadow became elated, leaping in its glass prison, laughing in its disquieting silent manner. The horizon drew closer and closer, bringing with it the deep rumble of tumbling water. A vast waterfall lay before them.

The crew frantically tried to steer the ship away, but great rocks either side of the vessel blocked their path. Captain Hake refused to allow his men to abandon ship. He ordered them to entangle themselves in the rigging, tie down the cannons and to hold on as tightly as they could.

"Finally!" He grinned, "After so many years. After so very many false leads and red herrings, I know where I am going. Following fragments of maps, half-remembered dreams, and conversations with mad men haunted by hallucinations; all pieces of this jigsaw course I plot. I will find you, Boy. I will take back my children."

"But Captain!" Cried out the Boatswain, "We are sure to crash into rocks below the waterfall and perish!"

"Nonsense, Smee! This is no common waterfall! This is the edge of the world!"

Laughing loudly, Captain Hake steered his ship over the rim. The Shadow, gleeful and leaping, pointed through the salt spray and churning mist. Two bright glimmers of light. Stars. Hake held fast to the wheel as the ship was spun about, tossed and turned, flipped and slapped about by the surging, falling waters. He heaved the wheel, and the sails caught a strange wind, filling, pulling and straining on their ropes. The Jolly Roger launched from the tumult into the calm darkness beyond the edge of the world. Stars above as below, and the slowly fading roar of the falls.

Before long the sun rose, pink and lemon-yellow through striped and stippled clouds. They found themselves sailing on a mirror-like sea. Still but for the breaking of the bow and the wake of the ship. It reflected the sky above it, clouds and birds in perfect symmetry. In the midst of this vast still mirror sat an island. Tall in the centre, steep and crooked and draped in a fine cloak of lush green foliage it reached out in many directions into the sea like the tentacles of a vast stone octopus. Sandbanks rose up treacherously here and there while unseen reefs threatened to tear slashes across the hull. Just offshore they dropped anchor, and prepared their row-boats to go ashore.

***

82

The Neverland was found to be plentiful of fruit and flower, and diverse in its array of monkeys and parrots and miscellaneous fringed lizards. They ate well, drank well, and began to forget why they had even made the journey to this odd isle. This was the strange power of The Neverland. It made you forget. After a time Captain Hake forgot about his wife, and their many happy years together. He began to forget about his children. Yet he would always recall that he sought a Boy. A terrible, naughty, horrid little Boy. The only things that would remain clear in the heads of the Pirates would be the happenings of recent days, and who they were, and what they were. And so one day they forgot about the Shadow, and unlocked its glass prison. It slipped away in the night, unseen and unheard.

The Shadow did not forget, for a shadow never forgets, and this Shadow belonged to Peter Pan, and when at last it was reunited with him it told him where it had been, and who had held it prisoner.

No matter how the Boy tried, his shadow would never be attached as firmly as once it was. Not by the application of soap, not by stamping on it, not by knotting it about his waist, not by laying on it and rolling up in it like a blanket. Nothing kept it secure any longer. As a punishment, Peter decided this vile Captain must lose something of his own.

Peter Pan; the lonely Boy kept about him a band of comrades he called his Lost Boys. In truth many were not lost at all, but stolen. They had each been taken in a similar manner to the children of James Hake; Minnie and Stanley.

What of those children? Stanley now called himself Slightly, as it is the last word he could recall his Mother saying to him. Why she said it, he did not know. Minnie had gone from the messy and unruly and smelly boys to join a tribe of Lost Girls on the far side of the Island. She too had selected a new name for herself; TigerLilly, and no longer knew that she had a brother, let alone a Mother or a Father.

Peter was the Boy who forbade growing up, and the curse of The Neverland kept him and his stolen friends young and playful and ignorant of all they left behind them, which suited Peter perfectly.

He could play and laugh and jump and fly and argue and go on mighty fine adventures with his troop of Lost Boys every day, and fill his hollow heart with wonder. But days and adventures end, and the crushing emptiness would fold over him like night over the evening sky.

The Lost Boys and their leader hatched a cunning plan. They taunted the Pirates with fly-by battles. Brief attacks and retreats. They pelted them with rotten eggs and stinky balls of mud. They lured them from their ship, and into a dangerous swamp.

Trees grew with great arching roots above the water, and slime grew on rocks like moss. It was in this tangle of roots and branches and slime that the Lost Boys and Peter Pan ambushed the Pirates.

Cutlas' clashed with clubs, fists met ribs and slingshots rattled marbles off of the Pirate's heads. Bows fired arrows from the treetops as a vicious rain.

"They're not children!" Cried out one of the Pirates, "They're cackling demons for sure!"

Peter Pan flew nimbly in circles around Captain Hake, who attempted to best the boy with elegant twirls and jabs with his vicious and hungry sword. With every lunge, the boy laughed and moved easily from the path of danger, flicking water with his toe-tips at Hake's now very bearded face.

The Captain, his trousers and boots waterlogged, his swashbuckling thoroughly impotent, tiring, was caught unawares by the boy and his swift dagger.

Peter latched onto Hake's sword-hand, and with one swift motion severed it from the wrist. Bone and sinew and tendon snapped, and the Captain's face became as pale as a sheet. Peter discarded Hake's sword, and launched away from the startled Captain, taking his twitching appendage with him.

"My hand!" Hake gasped, staring not at the boy, but at the space his hand once occupied at the end of his arm.

"You took my shadow. I have taken your hand. Are we even, now?" Peter laughed.

Crowing like a cockerel, the Boy spoke to his fairy friends, who awoke a nearby log. This driftwood creature paddled its long green tail side-to-side, reared up on its small hind legs, and moaned happily at the prospect of a free meal. Peter tossed Hake's hand into the mouth of the vast crocodile. The Pirates fled, taking their wounded Captain with them on their backs. All the while, the great green beast followed them, licking its long lips.

Many times over the weeks that followed did the crocodile attempt to finish its meal. On one such occasion it managed to rock the ship so violently that it listed far enough for it to launch its great scaly body onto the deck. Pirates scattered here and there, hacking at it with swords and poles and hatchets. Nothing could penetrate its thick driftwood hide. It opened its mouth to chomp down upon a terrified Pirate, but did not. The rakish angle at which the ship was pitching set free all manner of items, and into the crocodile's mouth slid a huge ornate clock. Down in one it went. Gulp!

With an upset tummy, the crocodile slunk away, followed by the dull ticking of the timepiece in its belly. Hake's recovery was long and arduous. He craved his lost hand, and to slay the Boy who had taken it from him. Around the ship, on all embankments, beaches and approaches that a croc may use, the Pirates lay great steel traps. Metal teeth that were ready to snap shut on the unsuspecting reptile.

Never once was it caught, as it was a crafty beast, and too clever to be outsmarted by mere man.

As replacement for his severed extremity Smee fashioned his Captain a savage metal hook! This was a weapon fit to take the life of the wretched flying Boy, and disband his loathsome troupe of Lost Boys. So Captain James Hake gave himself a new name. He would now be known as Captain Hook.

And so time wore on, heavy and monotonous, like the ticking of the clock in the belly of the croc which forever circled the Jolly Roger. The Pirates would attack the Lost Boys.

Then Lost Boys would retaliate against the Pirates. The Pirates would seek revenge. The Lost Boys would play tricks on the Pirates. On and on and on these adventures repeated. Weeks, months, years and decades became immaterial.

Step by step by tiny pigeon-step Hook and his Pirates came closer and closer to finding Pan's hidden lair, and to squashing his Lost Boys like bugs beneath boots.

Then one day, everything changed. The Boy brought to The Neverland a girl who refused to forget, and who refused to stay, and who reminded the Lost Boys of what a Mother was.

For the first time in many many years the Lost Boys began to think of the Mothers they left behind. Wendy's revolution spread to the Pirates once she and the Lost Boys were captured. The Pirates found her fascinating, and Hook became mesmerised by her stories. He was reminded of his Mother, and then he was reminded of the Mother of his children. Finally, he was reminded of his children.

A dread chill crept upon him as he recalled the many battles he had fought against the Lost Boys and the Lost Girls, and his own Minnie and Stanley that were counted among their number. He blamed the Boy for the curse of The Neverland, and vowed to rip him into pieces.

"That craven child will perish upon my vile barbed hook for all that he has done to me! For all that he has taken from me!"

Yet the Boy did not perish. Captain Hook died old and grey and withered and desperate. He more than any of his shipmates recalled all that he had lost, and in the remembering, undid the curse of The Neverland that prolonged their lives in forgetting.

James Hake remembered every day, every mistake, every friend left behind. More than anything else he remembered his wife and children, and this unbound him from the agelessness of this strange Island beyond the edge of the world. He creased up and folded like a deflating accordion, as the ravages of an ancient age fell upon him in a matter of days.

Wendy and her brothers left The Neverland, and so once more everyone forgot. Everyone except Hook, who shrivelled more and more into a pitiful raging husk.

His anger and sorrow an impotent flame burning itself into nothing. In this weakened state Pan found it easy to slip into his room and steal from his arm the feared hook.

He crowed and laughed and danced about as Hook expended the last of his energy in a chase to reclaim his property. He did not succeed.

Later that same day is when Smee discovered his Captain had died, caught in the teeth of a trap meant for the great beastly crocodile, a withered corpse of nothing more than bones and dry skin in moth eaten clothes.

The Pirates dug a grave and buried what remained of their Captain in it, erecting a makeshift headstone over the site. They returned to their ship, and forgot him.

The Lost Boys and the eternal Pan laughed and danced upon the grave, triumphant in their victory, then they too forgot all about him.

"What shall we do today, Peter?" Asked Slightly, the following morning.

"Why, it's time for another mighty fine adventure, I'd say. Come on Lost Boys, who's for a daring raid upon a Pirate Ship, recently moored upon our shores?"

The End

I Shall Wear Socks

In a strange and faraway land a young Maiden sobbed upon her bed. She wept for her father, who perished suddenly after remarrying to a beautiful but vile-tempered woman. There was no other family to offer the Maiden comfort, for her mother had passed away some years ago, and she was an only child.

Now the arch widower and her two terrible and treacherous daughters, bloated by inheritance and arrogance, uprooted the Maiden and took her away to a new and alien place. Here the Maiden shed her tears, crates all about her full of fine clothes and hats and dresses. Only one small chest amongst these riches was hers. She slowly picked through her chest dwelling on letters from her father, and discovering a diary she wrote when small.

Taking up her pen she began to write once more on the dry and yellowed pages of the diary.

Friday 10th January

Dear diary… do people even really say that when writing stuff in a journal? Is it one of those cliched things that only happens in films and on tv? Just a trope? Anyway, I thought I'd start up writing my diary again, as it's been a few years.

We've moved into the new house, it's still a mess of boxes, and I haven't found a job yet, but Trish and Tina told me about this website where weird old men pay them for their used underwear and socks and the like. Might give it a look over and see if I can't flog any of my stanky old leggings for a few bob to tide me over until I get a couple of gigs lined up or a permanent job.

Thanks for listening, Diary, my old pal. It's been good to catch up. Mwah!

   The wicked step-mother demanded much of the poor Maiden, while she sat back on plush cushions, drinking expensive red wine and eating delicate food in large slobbering bites. The step-sisters, believing themselves to be members of high society and ever so delightful and witty, had gentlemen callers at all hours. These poor unfortunate men often fled soon after arriving, fearful for their lives under the clawing grasping pink talons the sisters possessed in place of hands.

   Sunday 12th

What. A. Bitch.

   "What are you doing there, idling with that notebook?" The step-mother's voice was sharp as nails upon a blackboard.

93

"Make yourself useful!"

Poking fun at their poor step-sister, the ugly siblings tripped her and pulled at her hair, laughing all the while.

Monday 13th

Finally finished unpacking. It was my job to unpack for EVERYONE for some reason.

I knew she was a bit of a stuck up cow when she got with Dad, but since the accident she's got worse and worse. Now we're here, and Dad's not around, it's worse than ever. Feel a bit like a slave.

The sooner I can save up and get my own place the better!

The poor Maiden found an escape in her dreams and in her fantasies. She twirled about her room, singing to the woodland creatures that gathered to watch. So sweet was her voice, and so deeply she felt for the world around her, that they could not resist the lure of her.

Doe and fox and eagle and sparrow and wolf and bear and otter and vole watched through her window, finding there a peace and a happiness lacking in the wild places in which they dwelt.

94

Tuesday 14th

Unpacked all my makeup and dresses and wigs last night and had a little play. Got the slap on and did a quick Facebook Live lip sync routine. Donna Summer and Katy Perry with a little Sunset Boulevard thrown in. Got just over 100 viewers, and loads of nice comments from the old Drag Fam. I miss them so much already. Need to get out and see what the scene's like round here.

Miss Fortune will blow the local houses DOWN! Yaaas Kween!

    From her vigil each night, looking across the local town from her small window, she found herself alone, abandoned and ignored. If she maintained silence and hid herself away the vile step-family would sometimes forget that she even lived with them in that vast and empty house!
    Each evening the sound of laughter and bright chatter reached the Maiden's ears from the town. She wished that she might escape her isolation and servitude to revel in happy company and jolly people once again. But her clothes were as rags, and her hands and face grey from the scrubbing and cleaning she was forced to do at the behest of the wicked step-mother.

Thursday 16th

Ok so in order to go out this weekend I need some cash! Quick! Utterly skint is an understatement, and my bitch of a step-mum said I can have bugger all from her. A bit of a piss-take when she showers the two T's with wads of cash every other day. They really don't need that many handbags. Plus those extensions are SHOCKING! I could have done a better job for them but nooooooooooooo!

Signed up to that website today. Don't want it to be super obvious who I am, so think I'll just start off with foot photos or something. Loads of people are into feet. Isn't Tarantino into feet? Called myself twinkletoes_boy. Wonder if I'll get anyone interested.

The Maiden would regularly sit upon her window ledge, dangling one sleek leg into the sunlight beyond. She hid the rest of her with the curtains, so as not to show her grimy and worn visage to passers by.

Friday 17th

Mama got dollar! Can't believe it! £60 for pictures and videos of my feet in only 1 day! Enough for a taxi into town & back and a few bevvies tomorrow night. Yaaaaaaas!

Think I'll go for a simple Hot Mess kinda look. Need to brush out my Britney Bitch wig and dust off the hotpants.

    One evening, resolute in no longer being held prisoner, the Maiden preened and prepared herself as best she could. She wrapped herself in her cleanest dress and brushed at her hair with a fork.

    Tip-toeing through the house she was given away by a floorboard creaking a protest at her passing. The step-mother cried out and shrieked and forbade the poor Maiden from leaving her room.

Saturday 18th

I HATE her so fucking much! Locked me in my room so I couldn't go out. Threatened her with phoning the police, but my phone was on charge downstairs so I couldn't. I should be on a dance floor right now living it up!

She said I looked a state. She's one to talk! She just doesn't get Drag.

I miss Dad so much. He understood. He was proud of me for going out and living my truth. I've cried so much my eyelashes have come unstuck.

One summer day a handsome Prince was riding by and noticed the Maiden's leg protruding from the window and her dainty toes wiggling in the sun.

"Fair Maiden, your delicate porcelain toes are a delight. May I cast my eyes upon the rest of your form, sure to be quite beautiful and sublime?"

She pulled herself within as fast as she could, embarrassed, and hid away in the darkness of her lonesome room.

Sunday 19th

Got chatting to one of the young Daddies on FetTrade.com

He seems nice and was being sympathetic and supportive. I told him a bit about my situation. He's also quite fit, at least from the neck down, and into leather and rubber and all that. He's bought a couple of my foot photos to help me save up to move out. I think he's into feet too, but he could just be buying them to be nice.

Monday 20th

Job hunting sucks arse.

Entranced by the Maiden at the window, the Prince would often ride by the big house, hoping to catch a glimpse of the figure who lingered, hidden at the window. He longed to know her, and to converse with her, and spend time in the flowered summer meadows.

But he was a Prince! His parents expected greatness from him, and for him to marry a Princess from a neighbouring realm. The idea of such a union upset him and hurt him to his very heart. He followed his emotions, not tradition, and was displeased by all the ill-tempered and catty Princesses that thus far he had been introduced to. None of them did he find pleasing.

Friday 24th

Spent loads of time chatting to PrinceAlbert94 again yesterday. Sent me a couple more pics of him in his gear. Still no face pic. He's in the closet! I came out when I was a tadpole.

Apparently it's a cultural thing, his parents expect him to marry a woman and have kids and all that boring hetero shit. I told him I did Drag, so I could pretend to be his

99

girlfriend and his parents would never know. He found it funny. I should think so too. I'm hilarious!

The terrible step sisters found the Maiden to have skills in dressing and hair styling and in the application of paint and powder for the face. They cajoled and caroused her into pampering them for a night of merriment in the local town. The Maiden pulled their corsets too tight and brushed their hair quite viciously. All, said she, necessary to accentuate their beauty. It was some small amount of petty revenge that amused her for a while.

The sisters staggered from the house in pantomime dress, sure to be found ridiculous, the young Maiden thought happily.

Sunday 26th

The two T's went out last night and got wasted. I had to help them get dressed and do their hair and makeup. I only did it so they'd stop pestering me and leave me alone. Pair of fat slags. And their mum's no better. Like a side of pork in curlers. No amount of makeup can polish those turds.

Every afternoon the Maiden watched the Prince ride by upon his stallion. As he passed, she slipped out her leg, and he paused, calling to her to show her face so that they may speak and be introduced.

Monday 27th

PrinceAlbert94 is definitely into feet.

Tuesday 4th Feb

My life is just housework and chores now. The Bitches don't lift a finger.
I got mad and we had a huge argument. They ended up just laughing at me! I was so cross I trashed the kitchen. My punishment was to tidy up the mess, my phone taken off me, no Netflix. I was half way through binging Sabrina as well! How dare they interrupt my fix of camp witchy spookness with that sexy Satan.

Good job they don't know about my old Ipad. Ha!

Messaged the Drag Fam for a kiki. It was so nice to talk to them again. This Zoom app is great! Nancy and Bell have got new gigs at the club twice a month, and little Drag sis Smokey has started a wig styling business

from the back of his camper van. Love that little weirdo.
Mama Mank said she'd put me in touch with someone
local to take me out. She's got contacts.

Went online for a little sexy 'self care' and ended up on
FetTrade again. PrinceAlbert94 said there's a Ball
coming up soon. Apparently the local Drag and Fetish
scenes have a bit of a cross-over and this big Ball once a
year is for everyone freaky to let loose and have a blow out
and a blow job, if they're lucky. Told him I probably
wouldn't be able to go because of being under house arrest.
He seemed a bit sad about that.

Our chats sometimes get a little cheeky. If he gets too
forward I tell him "behave, or I shall wear socks, and
you'll not see my lovely feet!'"

He's a lot of fun. Quite sweet really. Just wish I could see
his face. I sent him one of mine. I thought it might
encourage him to loosen up a bit and show me his face. He
wouldn't. Too worried and shy and all that. He said he
envies my confidence and balls. Not that he's seen them.
He meant bravado I think.

     The Maiden's invitation to the Ball was held aloft
by the wicked step-mother, who spat as she spoke. She was
in a rage that the Maiden dare to think of leaving the

house. She was in a fury that she dare to even think of attending such an event!

Saturday 8th

So yesterday I might have let slip to Trish that I want to go out to the Sleaze Ball next week, and of course she told Her Bitchness Most High. Guess who kicked off? She did! Told her what I thought of her, and she threw my dinner in the bin. I had only just sat down to eat it! Fucking bitch.

Had a sulk and Zoomed the Drag Fam again. We had a 5 way dance-off, music nice and loud! Completely pissed off the T's and She Who Must Not Be Named, but that was part of the fun. The Fam made me feel loads better. Now I need to plan my outfit.

I. Will. Go. To. The. Ball!
Might dip into the Foot Fund for a new outfit. What did people do before online shopping?

Foaming at the mouth with a rabid rage, the wicked step-mother tossed the Maiden's invitation to the Ball upon the fire.

103

"You shall never attend the Ball! You stinking, ugly, vile child! The very idea! You'd make a show of yourself and disgrace us for sure."

Wednesday 12th

Welcome to Tension Central! The step-family has been making it SUPER awkward this week. Hiding my packages. Idiots! I got tracking info! I know you signed for them!

PrinceAlbert94 says he's looking forward to meeting me at the Ball. I asked how I'd recognise him, as I've never seen his face. He said he'd find me. I'm getting a little nervous about it now. I don't know anyone here aside from him. And I don't REALLY know him. Just his online persona.

This could be a huge mistake.

Mama Mank said she'd sort me out. No idea what she's talking about. Probably pissed.

Friday 14th

Bitches still won't tell me where they've hidden all my new stuff. Gonna turn this house upside down if I have to!

The Maiden looked to disobey her wicked step-mother, and she asked the woodland animals that gathered at her window what she might do. How might she avoid discovery in her exit of the house, and what might she wear, as all her clothes were tatters and rags!

Saturday 15th

I can't decide what to wear. I can't decide if I should even go to the Ball tonight!

Dad would tell me to stop overthinking everything, live in the moment and enjoy it for what it is.

Not sure if I can.

Sparkling magic filled the air, and from the vapours emerged a Fairy God Mother and her pixie apprentices.

They comforted the Maiden, and promised that she would indeed attend the Ball.

The Fairy God Mother waved her wand and sang a spell that wove fabric from the air, and it shone like glass reflecting candlelight. The poor Maiden was transformed!

The Maiden did indeed attend the Ball, taken there in a fine carriage, where she danced with Lords and Ladies, and briefly found herself in the company of the handsome Prince!

At the striking of the clock, the Maiden fled, fearing the late hour. She would need to be home and at work in short shrift, as her wicked step-mother demanded her chores begin early, before even the morning chorus of the birds.

Sunday 16th

Guuuuurl! We slayed the house DOWN!

I can't believe it! The Drag Fam turned up on my doorstep. They all got a lift in Smokey's little camper, arrived in full Drag, terrified the step-monsters into giving up all my hidden treasure and did me up a treat!

We hit the town in our highest heels, biggest wigs, cinched to the Gods and we served them boys a vision of Kinky Latex Queen realness the like of which they'd never seen!

I think I spoke to PrinceAlbert94, but he didn't really give himself away or introduce himself properly. I think he was a bit intimidated. If it was him. It might not have been him. I hope it was him. He was hot hot hot!
Mama Mank, Bell, Nancy and Smokey all crashed in my room with me. There is glitter on EVERYTHING and it is faaaaaabulous. I think I lost a shoe at the Ball, and Smokey certainly lost her dignity. Never seen someone try and slip a finger in quite that publicly before. So thirsty.

Tuesday 18th

It was sad to say bye to the Drag Fam yesterday. Promised them I'd visit soon with my new found foot wealth.

PrinceAlbert94 messaged me. He was nervous about talking to me at the Ball, he didn't know what to say. So happy! It WAS him I spoke to. He's cute, we can chat for hours, and he's into some right sexy shenanigans. Fun!

Seems he found my lost shoe. I told him he can keep it as a memento.

The Prince, who had fallen deeply in love with the Maiden during their encounter at the Ball, searched the kingdom high and low for the owner of the shoe she left behind. Every foot found itself to be too big, or too narrow, or too crooked, or too wide. He despaired that he might never find his love.

Friday 21st

The worst few days ever. The T's have been making constant snide comments. They're such 'phobes. Water off a duck's back. Water off a duck's back.

I had a little cry last night, missing Dad like crazy. It's been months since he died, but it's still so raw. I try not to think about it too much.

Not heard from PrinceAlbert94 since Tues. Hope seeing me in Drag didn't put him off.

I'm still selling loads of pics and vids on FetTrade, and in a few months I'll have enough for a deposit for a little studio apartment I found on Gumtree. One room with a bed, oven and space for a TV, and a cupboard that's been made into a bathroom. It won't be anything special, but it'll be mine. Eventually. That's if it's even still available then!

Need out of here NOW!

The Prince's search was coming to a close, and suddenly he recalled the Maiden at the window, and thought of her foot, and of the shoe in his possession. Could it be that they were one and the same person?

Saturday 22nd

Shit off! I can't even! No way! My life cannot get any fucking weirder!

Guess who turned up at the front door last night? PrinceAlbert94! Even out of his skimpy outfits he was damn fine. Just a tshirt and jeans but they hugged in all the right places. Finger lickin' chicken!
He had my bloody shoe with him too.

It turns out Mama Mank messaged him. They'd been chatting at the Ball, and she worked out who he was. She found him on Facebook, did a bit of stalking, then messaged him my address!

He called me twinkletoes, it was cute. I asked him if he
had honorable intentions. He said he might.
I told him to treat me well, or I shall wear socks, and he
won't get to see my lovely feet.

Aaaaanyway, he was a sweetheart. Took me out for a meal
at an expensive Thai place he knew. I lost track of the
time, and didn't fancy having to go home and face down
the Bitches of Eastwick. So I didn't stay home last night.

I don't think I'll ever wear socks again.

The Prince and the Maiden kissed, slipped on their
rings, and they were wed. The crowd cheered and threw
coloured paper into the air. Bluebirds flew about them and
sang, while the animals of the wild places cavorted merrily.
The whole kingdom rejoiced!
And they lived happily ever after.

THE END

A Circus Of Decay

The Farmer scratched his head, confused. His vast sheep fields that yesterday had been home to his award winning flock were now occupied by a sprawling circus. The dawn chorus had only recently begun to sound, and the Farmer could not understand how such a vast and complicated construction like this circus could have been erected without any noise whatsoever.

He and his wife were both very light sleepers, and the slightest unfamiliar sound would awaken them. Yet last night they had slept very soundly, and here in his fields there lay a circus that had not been there the day before.

Centrally stood the big top, a wide circular tent in yellow and green striped fabric. Arranged in huddled clusters around this central hub were smaller tents, shuttered food trucks, the slumbering forms of mechanical funfair rides, and cages in which slept strange exotic animals from far overseas.

"How odd." Said the farmer, calling his dog to his side, "Where are the sheep?"

In an effort to rid his farm of the inconvenience of a circus and the countless hordes it was sure to attract, the Farmer strode into the tangle of tents and silent attractions, calling out for the Ringmaster, or the owner, or some similar such person.

Alongside the sound of his feet, and the padding of his dog's paws there was occasionally another sound. Something just on the edge of hearing.

"Is there someone there?" He spun around to where he thought the noises might be originating.

A shapeless shadow slipped quickly away from his gaze.

"Hello?"

The birds were no longer singing. The air was still, and the Farmer found himself becoming uncommonly alarmed.

"Come along, Tess." He said to his dog.

The animal stood with her tail between her legs. She looked about nervously, before yapping once and running, full sprint, back to the farmhouse.

The Farmer shouted after the dog, but was ignored by the scared animal. Shaking his head, he returned his attention to the circus around him. Once again some formless dark shape slid into hiding at the corner of his eye.

Passing a cage lined with straw, he looked upon the sign staked into the soft ground; *The Blood Thirsty Chupacabra*. Peering closer, the Farmer saw the spine of some mangey animal nestled out of sight amongst its bedding. 'Likely just some poor hairless dog or cat done up like a freak-show attraction', the Farmer thought of the pitiful little shape.

He turned to move away from the cage, and - *HONK* - yelped in shock at a clown stood mere inches behind him. How had he approached so silently, with shoes that big? The clown squeezed his nose again, sounding off a second loud honk.

His face was painted with a thick and cracked layer of white greasepaint, upon which an exaggerated smile had been drawn in red. His hair was a bright red wig, upon the top of which perched a tiny top hat.

"Oh, hello." Said the Farmer, "I'm looking for whoever's in charge. I'm Arthur, by the way. "

The clown cocked its head to one side, his small dark eyes puckering at the sides as he gave a very wide and open smile.

"You're trespassing on my property." The Farmer continued. "You need to pack up and clear off or I'll summon the coppers to move you on."

The clown turned and walked away, his waddling comical gate accentuated by his big round belly of padding and overlong shoes. After a few paces he paused, when he realised Arthur was not following. He beckoned with a gloved hand that he should be accompanied.

'Hopefully', the Farmer thought, 'this daft man will take me to someone in charge!'

The waddling clown led the Farmer to the Big Top, and vanished inside the closed flaps of the entrance. Lifting one of the heavy pieces of striped canvas cautiously, the Farmer called into the darkness and musk beyond the small pool of illumination in front of him.

"Hello in there? I'm here about your Circus being on my land."

He received no reply, so stepped inside.

Several hours later, the Farmer's wife noted that her husband had not been back to the house for his customary cup of tea and peanut butter sandwich at lunch time. She peered out of the window at the Circus, and scanned the grounds.

"Where has Arthur got to?" She muttered to herself.

She watched a gaggle of discordantly coloured clowns emerge from the Big Top and make themselves busy in the opening of the food trucks and the lighting of the many many electric bulbs that were strung up like fallen stars as a canopy above the Circus.

Word spread fast throughout the town that a circus had set up overnight at a nearby farm. Those who did not find out through hearsay discovered it by the great many posters that appeared nailed to fences and doors and telegraph poles throughout the course of the day.

As the afternoon waned, and the warm summer evening cast it's muggy shadow across the town, people finished their chores and readied themselves for a night at the circus! Families and courting couples and lonesome men and women began to make their way toward the distant sound of music, and the harsh glow of the electric lights.

"What happens at a circus?" Asked one of a pair of identical small girls, skipping at their mother's side.

"All manner of things, Abigail!" Her mother thought back to her own experience of attending a circus show in the City when young, "Fantastical feats of acrobatics, tamed foreign animals, and clowns! Oh such funny tumbling clowns!"

Little Abigail clapped happily. Her and her twin Winifred began to imagine all kinds of magical and miraculous things that they might see, eager for the evening's entertainment.

The queue at the entrance was long and winding, but even here folk were not left bored or unentertained. Jugglers and fire breathing women strode amongst the crowd, wowing with their skills and displays.

Balls of fire shot from the women's mouths, adding a frisson of danger and surprise to the waiting masses. The jugglers took items from the crowd and tossed them skilfully to one another, over the heads of the onlookers. Watches and hats and even a false leg were added to the wooden pins already airborne.

"Admittance for one, please." Said a young man by the name of Jimmy.

He wore his nicest clothes and had slicked his hair. Clearly he hoped to find someone to court while at the circus. He breathed into his hand and sniffed, finding the aroma not displeasing.

"You are here on your own?" The crone at the counter handed him his ticket, her one good eye inspecting him closely.

Jimmy nodded, saying that he had snuck out to attend the circus. His parents were devout and did not approve of the fripperies and frivolities associated with a place like this.

"Be sure to visit Mystic Meem. She can read your fortune. Maybe love is on the cards for you? Good luck."

He smiled eagerly, and said that he would. She patted his hand and shooed him away, so that the next in line may be served.

Two ladies of indeterminate age held hands as they walked slowly from a wagon where they purchased a hot dog and a bag of popcorn. They shared the hot dog, laughing as the slimmer of the two spilled bright yellow mustard onto her jumper.

"Oh Laura! You dafty."

The couple wiped away the mustard and began to share the popcorn, watching a group of small people perform comically bad gymnastic routines upon a circular stage.

"Are we allowed to call them midgets anymore?" Laura asked of her partner, who shrugged.

"I don't know. Why?"

Laura pointed to a wooden sign staked into the ground. In bold black painted letters it proclaimed the troupe to be the *Midget Gems, tumbling acrobats from a forgotten isle off the coast of India*.

"Looks like a very old fashioned circus, this." Observed Hayley, "Maybe see if we can't just enjoy it for what it is?"

They watched the Gems perform stunt after well-rehearsed failing stunt. Laura and Hayley chuckled along with the others who watched this side show.

"They're very talented." Hayley said, as she finished the popcorn.

***

117

Mildred, the Farmer's wife, watched the massing crowd from her kitchen window. Arthur had been missing since going to see about the circus first thing in the morning. She had waited and fretted all day, unsure what she should do.

As the main lights of the circus had been lit, and as the funfair rides had begun to spin, she picked up her phone, and spun the dial round to 9 three times. The rapid clicking of the spinning device ended in a low crackling buzz in the earpiece. She dialled again, with a similar lack of success.

The phone line was down. She would have to venture out either to the police station, or into the circus for herself. She did not much fancy leaving the farm unattended with so many people milling about. She left Tess the dog inside, and went out into the close and humid summer evening.

Luckily, due to the orientation of the circus and the approach of the road up to the farm, from the house she arrived at the circus from the rear. She moved slowly into the glare of the suspended circus lights, hoping that amongst the crowd she might find an off duty Bobby, whose ear she could bend.

She bumped into someone, and was taken aback by the sheer size of them. She had walked into a Strong Man display, and interrupted his poses and strutting. Mildred apologised, and moved to back away, but the Strong Man had a cheeky glint in his eye.

"Who wants to see me lift this lady?" He called loudly to the crowd watching him.

Mildred was not small, and suspected he was having her on. She smiled shyly and attempted to hurry away. The crowd had cheered at his suggestion, and so he stooped, swept her up and lifted her bodily up into the air over his head. The crowd applauded and several women fanned themselves more rapidly than they had already been doing, making gentle 'oh' sounds as they did so.

Next, Mildred was slung over the man's wide shoulders in a fireman's lift, and he spanked her bottom playfully before setting her down and thanking her for being a good sport.

Bright red with embarrassment, Mildred scurried away.

Between the food carts and small tents holding side-show attractions Jimmy was weaving a zigzag path. There was a girl at school whom he admired from afar, and knew that she would be at the circus with her friends. He hoped to spot them in the crowd, and to make himself noticed by her, so that he could begin a conversation. He found that at school he was always too nervous, and stuttered and failed to speak. Here amongst the anonymous crowd however, he felt braver that no one would judge him if he made a goof of himself.

They mustn't have arrived yet. Good, he had beaten them to it. He could pick his spot and wait to be noticed, standing casually against here, or leaning there maybe?

As he scoped out good locations, he stumbled upon the striped tent outside of which stood the sign for

Mystic Meem, fortune teller. He supposed he could waste some time and a couple of bob on having his palm read, or whatever it was that fortune tellers told a fortune by.

There was no line for this tent, and so he let himself in. The interior was black and thick with incense. The heat inside the tent was oppressive, and the smell of burned herbs made his head spin.

"Come, boy. Sit."

Mystic Meem stepped from the shadows and into the light of the single candle. Now that his eyes were adjusting to the dim illumination, he could make out a small table arranged with two chairs in the middle of the space on a threadbare Persian rug.

She wore veils and golden bangles, her nose and ears were pierced, and her hair was black as coal.

"You would like to know your fortune?"

He shrugged, "Suppose."

She held out a hand to one of the chairs. Both the chair and her hand were painted with red lines in intricate swirling patterns. She was quite beautiful, but likely much older than she looked, he thought.

Sitting in the chair, he was circled by the Mystic. Her fingertips grazed his shoulder as she passed, and he felt an electric charge sweep through him at their touch.

Eventually she sat, and examined his face.

"Cards, tea, crystal or palm?" She asked, nodding to a paper sign that informed him of the price for each reading.

He clumsily handed her the three shillings that a palm reading would cost, and she slipped the coins into some hidden purse or pocket.

She took his hands in hers, turning them both over so they faced palm up.

"The left shows your potential, your possible, your future." She squeezed his left hand ever so slightly, "The right," She squeezed, "What you have done with that potential, which deeds lead to the future laid before you."

He was skeptical of magic and similar 'mumbo jumbo', so he said nothing, and waited to hear what she had to say.

She leaned in, working her eyes across the lines of one hand, onto the other and back again. Presently she sat back, but remained holding onto his hands.

"There is a girl." Said she, "Do not pursue her. It will lead to unhappiness and misery, never being settled or secure."

Jimmy tried to pull his hands back, but Meem clutched them and would not give.

"There are two potentials, two possibles, two futures I see. Both are sad, but in different ways. Follow the girl, misery and fear. Give up that chase, boredom and regret and loathing."

Jimmy finally freed his hands from her tight grip, "Ok, thanks. Is that everything?"

She sat back in her chair, folding her arms. In the silence that followed, Jimmy thought he noticed some genuine concern cross her expression, but decided that he was done with this charlatan. He stood and pushed open the flaps of the tent.

"What I say is the truth." She called after him, "Choose wisely which path you walk! The fork in your road will appear tonight!"

Laura and Hayley paused briefly at an oversized puppet show, where grotesque marionettes jigged about to the music of a hidden barrel organ. Once they both admitted that they had no clue as to what the story was the puppets were telling, they moved on.

The smell of fresh manure and straw tugged at Laura's nose. She was a veterinarian, and so concerned herself greatly with the welfare and good treatment of animals. Dragging Hayley with her, she approached the semi-circle of cages which housed the circus' more obscure beasts.

The first cage was marked as containing a Chupacabra, but Laura knew that what lay shivering and growling in the cage was a dog, long suffering with mange and clouded cataracted eyes. It appeared malnourished, as the lumps of its spine were clearly visible along its back.

"Poor thing." She said, "If I could get it to the surgery it'd be healed and healthy in a matter of weeks."

The sign at the next cage read *Bishop-Fish*. In the roof of this cage a rudimentary sprinkler system had been installed, which intermittently sprayed a mist of water down upon its occupant. Laura squinted through the water haze, unsure if she could make out the creature. It sat hunched like a man, its back to her, hugging its knees.

It seemed to sense Laura and Hayley's proximity, and turned its domed head to peer at them with large dark eyes. Laura gasped and pulled back from the cage. The Bishop-Fish was blue-green in colour, with dappled black markings across its rounded body. It was covered in scales, and what Laura had mistaken for flowing fabric about its shoulders were in fact long and prehensile fins like that of a lion fish.

It lifted one human-like hand, made the sign of the Christian cross across itself, and began to recite the Lord's Prayer in a low and gurgling voice.

"What was that?" Hayley asked.

She had held back from the cage, and so did not get as full a view as her partner. Laura shook her head, unsure. They moved onto the next cage.

Unicorn; read this sign.

"No way!" Hayley laughed, doubtful that such a plainly fictitious creature could possibly exist.

A shaggy black horse could clearly be seen inside this cage, which was far too small for it to be comfortable. Its head was bent down so that it could eat the straw of its bedding. Hayley pushed a hand in through the bars and slapped the animal's behind.

"Turn round! Let us see your horn!"

The animal lifted its head, and snorted. The women gasped, for sure as they were stood there, this horse had a horn growing from the middle of its forehead. The horn was crooked and twisted, scratched and scarred in places. It was not the thing of beauty they had imagined.

The unicorn turned slowly around to face Laura and Hayley, its horn rattling along the bars as it turned.

"It might be an abnormal growth, a cutaneous horn." Laura observed, "It can't be a real Unicorn, can it?"

But the Bishop-Fish remained in her thoughts, and she looked back at the preceding cages into which they had peered. Could these strange beasts be real?

They moved on to see what could possibly lay within the final cage in this display. *The Dog Faced Man of Madagascar*, proclaimed the sign.

"Well this is just going to be some rare, large Lemur." Laura said, hoping it to be true.

She did not like the idea of all she thought she knew and understood of the animal world being ripped up and tossed away before her eyes. Hayley moved to the cage first, and was silent, watching through the bars. Laura approached slowly, looking over her partner's shoulder warily.

Inside the cage sat three individuals. A male, a female, and a pup. These were not simply a family of large Lemurs, they were physically human, they moved like humans and their facial expressions moved like humans. But their bodies were covered in hair, with long tails protruding from the base of their spines. They had long snouts and ears on the top of their heads, still somewhat humanlike in shape, but more pointed at the top.

"I don't believe it." Laura breathed, "They can't be real. None of these can be real."

Sure that all of these displays were hokum, Laura moved quickly back to the cage marked Chupacabra. If she could examine that poor little animal and prove it was nothing more than a poorly Xoloti, or similar breed of dog she would feel much better. The doubt in her mind was festering, and she avoided looking into the cages of the Unicorn and Bishop-Fish as she passed them.

She knelt at the Chupacabra cage, and reached an arm inside.

"Come on little one. It's ok. Come and say hello. Come on, mama's not going to hurt you."

The animal reared up, hissing and snarling. As it rose, it became clear that this was no dog. It's back legs were long like a kangaroo, and a forked tongue flicked in and out of its mouth.

Hayley shouted for Laura to pull her arm from the cage, but she was too stunned to move. The animal lunged forward, biting onto the wrist held out to it with needle sharp teeth. Laura screamed, trying to pull herself free of the powerful bite. Hayley beat at the bars of the cage with her fists, shouting for someone to help.

No one helped, everyone stood and gawped.

Blood poured from Laura's wrist as the Chupacabra sucked at the wound its teeth made. Finally letting go, its clouded eyes glinting red, it moved to lapping up the spilled blood amongst its bedding.

Hayley took her hanky and bound Laura's wrist as tightly as she could. The wound looked yellow and infected already, making Laura shake all over with shock and fear.

From the startled crowd appeared a clown. The same round clown who had met with Arthur in the morning. He kindly helped Laura to stand, and she leant on him for support.

Hayley thanked the clown for his help, as he led them away.

Abigail and Winifred, hand in hand, skipped between the stalls and stands, goggle-eyed at all the colourful and miraculous things they saw. A man led a bear through the crowd on a chain, and it paused to dance for them, slow and ponderous. The girls giggled and danced around it, and away into the crowd.

Their mother was wrecked with worry, as they had vanished into the crowd and been lost to her. She called out their names, hurrying here and there. But they were lost in the maze of the circus.

A Tall man in a tall hat approached the happy girls, and said they looked wonderfully rosy and cheerful and full of glee. They giggled and curtseyed and said thank you.

"I am a magician," He told them, "Would you like to be in my act? I perform in the Big Top very soon."

Abigail and Winifred both said yes, hopping up and down in excitement.

Jimmy watched the girl he adored eating candy floss and laughing with her friends. She was beautiful. He pictured their first kiss, he imagined how sweet she would smell, and the press of her body against his. He positioned himself so that she could not hope but notice him as she walked by.

She approached. Her friends chatted and laughed, and he hoped they wouldn't distract her from seeing him. Then another boy appeared, and he took her hand, and she kissed him. Jimmy's heart sank as this unknown boy stole his love away.

Jimmy followed them. Passing behind carts and booths and tents, the couple hid themselves amongst some crates, where they began to become very intimate. Jimmy watched for a moment, shocked and angry, then turned and ran. He tripped over a guide rope and collapsed sideways into a long rectangular tent. He had fallen into the middle of the Snake Charmer's show, upsetting the basket from which a frilled cobra was slowly unwinding. The audience gasped, unsure if this was a part of the act or not.

The snake charmer, a curvaceous woman wearing little more than undergarments struck Jimmy with her flute. He apologised and apologised again. He stumbled as he stood, and tripped over the cobra in its basket once again. The angered animal hissed and struck at Jimmy, biting him swiftly and briefly upon the ankle.

Jimmy wailed as a jolt of pain shot through him, and he clutched at his injured leg. The snake struck again, this time of Jimmy's arm, then again on his face.

The charmer slammed the lid onto the basket, trapping the cobra inside, then quickly ushered her small audience out of the tent. She returned to Jimmy, and asked him how he was.

Jimmy could not reply, his lips were fat and numb, and his face tingled. His arms and legs began to feel loose and fell slack at his side. He slumped backwards onto the

127

floor, panic rising in his chest. The charmer stood over him, and he looked into her eyes, begging for help, but he was unable to make a sound.

      Hayley pushed the clown away from Laura.

      "Where the hell are you taking us?"

      The clown had led them around in circles. They were back at the row of caged beasts!

      "I thought you were taking her for medical attention!"

      The clown released Laura and shrugged, then skipped away into the crowd, honking his nose. Hayley lifted Laura and supported her as best she could, and they hurried from the circus.

      "Roll up, roll up, the Big Top show is about to begin!" The Ringmaster, tall and dark in a handsome red tailcoat bellowed from the entrance of the large tent that occupied the majority of the space in the circus. He shouted and hollered and tossed his cane in the air, drawing attention to the Big Top.

      A sea of happy smiling faces turned his way, and began to drift in through the open canvas flaps.

      Mildred, caught in the surge, found herself swept into the stalls in the front row of the tiered Big Top seating benches. She sat there, marvelling at the sheer number of people that were filing in and filling the space.

      When all the seats had been filled, and the entrance flaps closed, the lights within the big tent were dimmed. A small spotlight shone on a man, taking up position in a chair off-centre in the ring. He held a saw and a violin bow. He gripped the handle of the saw between his thighs, and bent the blade, running the bow along its blunt back edge. The sound was eerie, full of off tones and mysterious harmonies. It reminded Mildred of the sounds used instead of music in a lot of the science fiction movies Arthur liked to take her to watch in the cinema.

The Ringmaster materialised through a cloud of smoke in the centre of the ring, "Through the mists of time, and across countless lands we have travelled. From the very depths of the Peruvian jungle, to the highest peaks of the Himalayas." He went on and on, hinting at the wondrous things he had seen, "Today, we bring those miracles to you."

In another cloud of smoke the Ringmaster was gone. The musician lay down his saw and bow, stood, took a bow, then left the ring in darkness.

Mildred found herself very entertained by the lion tamer and the dancing bears. She uttered an incredulous 'wow' at the skills of the high-wire and trapeze acts.

The tiny tumblers, the snake charmer and strongmen she found entertaining enough, but she reminded herself that dear Arthur was still missing. She was sat here, enjoying herself, when anything could have happened to him!

Next there was a magic show, where a magician, who looked suspiciously like the Ringmaster performed the usual selection of tricks and misdirections.

For his final trick, he called two girls from the audience. They skipped into the ring and were each helped into an oblong box. Using the saw presented to him by the musician from the opening of the show, he began to saw the girls in two. The audience gasped as their feet continued to wiggle, and the girls laughed as they were smoothly and cleanly severed across the middle.

The halves were then rearranged on top of one another, then side by side and back to back, all for the audience to see the independent moving parts and the cheerful faces of the girls.

After a great show of apparent confusion in how to reassemble the girls, the magician succeeded, and the two happy children were whole again, took their bows, and were escorted backstage by the magician-come-Ringmaster.

The finale act was that of the clowns. They came jumping and tumbling into the ring, tripping each other, miming out great slapstick scenes, and causing great hilarity among the stalls.

One face remained impassive. Mildred watched one of the clowns closely. His face was painted white and his eyebrows drawn high on his forehead, giving him an almost sorrowful expression. There were three tufts of hair slicked out from his head, painted blue, and he wore an oversized coat and preposterous shoes. Mildred watched this clown as he cavorted and cartwheeled and pranced about.

It was Arthur!

When the show was finished the audience applauded and cheered at all the performers, parading around the ring for their bows. Mildred did not clap or cheer. She excused herself, squeezing past the people seated beside her and slipped into the backstage area of the Big Top

Mildred waited for the performers to retire to their various trailers and tents. She followed the clowns to their cart, and peered in one of the windows. Slowly they removed their makeup and clothes.

Beneath the greasepaint and powder their faces were gaunt, hollow and emaciated. Beneath their clothes were open and rotting wounds, and they spoke not a word to one another.

Arthur removed his costume, and revealed beneath his collar a deep gash in his neck. His throat had been slit, almost taking his head clean off, yet still he lived! Mildred gasped, slapping a hand over her mouth. The undead clowns reacted to the sound of her shock, and moved slowly from their cart.

Mildred backed away, tears filling her eyes, as the corpse of her husband came toward her, head lolling to one side. He held out one hand to her. She wanted to touch his hand, to hold him, for him to comfort her.

"Arthur?" She shivered.

Arthur did not respond.

The clowns advanced, and Mildred ran away.

The following day the vast fields lay empty, the grass and weeds trodden flat and brown. The circus had packed up and moved on overnight, unseen and unheard in its passing. Now the people turning up to experience another afternoon of fire breathers and lion tamers and jugglers and clowns and fairground rides faced nothing but a disappointing Sunday.

"Where has the circus gone?" Asked a small boy, sitting upon his father's shoulders.

A police car sat upon the drive leading to the farmhouse, and within, Mildred wept as she told the officers what she had seen.

The train car rattled and groaned as it rolled over old and uneven tracks. The heavy smell of animals and greasepaint filled the closed atmosphere, and the Ringmaster examined the newest members of his circus troop.

He made up signs for the two new additions to the Freak Show. Painstakingly he painted the letters in slow, careful sweeps of his brush. He paused now and again as the train juddered or shook.

Finished, he lay them out to dry:

The Human Statue. See his eyes move, yet the rest of him lays dormant and frozen! A victim of Medusa's legendary stare, and *The Two Headed Girl. A miracle of modern medicine, two heads, two hearts, but not a tongue between them with which to speak.*

Abigail and Winifred stirred from sleep, woozy from drugs and in exceptional agony. They reached for the other, and screamed wordlessly at how they found themselves; unzipped from chest to groin and sewn up into one body.

Jimmy watched, yet could do nothing, he could say nothing. His breaths were long and shallow, and his heart beat once every now and then, but his mind raced frantically like a hamster in a wheel. He tried to speak, to cry, to scream... But he was utterly impotent in all regards.

Arthur felt a maggot crawl from the floor and between his grey exposed toes. He watched it slowly begin to pick at his flesh, its tiny jaws pulling at the skin. Before long the creeping bug had created opening enough to push itself inside, making there a warm and tasty home within the slowly decaying flesh of Arthur's foot.

THE END

Little Stitches

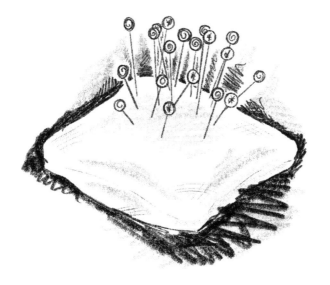

She began work in the Cotton Mill on her 6th birthday. Her Mother also worked at the Mill, but the young girl didn't ever see her during the long working hours. She spent her time beside the loud and rapidly moving machines, waiting to be told what to do, and avoiding the jeering and sniggering boys of her own age also employed as mule scavengers. They had worked there a good two years or so already, and knew what to do and when to do it. She couldn't often hear what they said over the noise of the machines, but she knew it was not kind. She had a lisp, and her back was slightly askew; easy pickings for the teasing boys. She hated her voice and the *th* sounds she couldn't help but make, and she hated her crooked spine. More than anything she wished to be normal and everyday and common-or-garden and not to stand out and be pitied like she so often was. But she knew wishes never came true, no matter what fairy tales promised.

Despite her mildly misshapen body, she was as spry and nimble as any of the others, and due to her small size was able to squeeze below the machines as they thrashed and heaved their mechanical arms too and fro. She was most frequently commanded to remove the buildup of dirt and detritus. Sometimes she rescued bundles of loose threads of precious cotton that could be reused. On one occasion she also had to fetch back the body of another child who had been in the way of one of the vicious and unrelenting mechanisms of the vast machine. His arm had been pulled clean off. There were no words that she knew to explain how the sight of that made her feel.

It was a dangerous life.

From time to time, while she avoided other children and waited to be told to once more get on her belly and crawl, she would gaze around the room, out of the grimy windows, or let her eyes loose focus and watch the strange rhythms and colours of the Mill churn around her.

Every day a magpie came to the window. It hopped along the narrow ledge, tilting its head one way then the other, examining the interior of the Mill with each eye in turn. She imagined him to be a noble gentleman in his fancy black and white suit, and so saluted him when he came by for his morning constitutional and gossip. She would tell him what the sniggering boys had been up to, and the jokes they had played on each other.

"They *th*at him upon a cushion full of pin*th*!" She laughed, remembering his yelp of surprise.

The boy of which she spoke was one of the worst of them, always poking her in the back and telling her to stand up straight, or asking her to say words that she found tricky. She was very glad when he was made to yowl like a wounded dog, and was not afraid to hide her smirk.

"Stop lollygagging! Stupid girl! Why stand there daydreaming when there's work to be done?"

The foreman often berated her.

At the end of the working days her Mother would take her hand and lead her home. They would cook and eat dinner in an exhausted silence, then fall into bed to sleep for too few hours, before the knocker-upper was round to rap on windows and they began their day anew.

"Come along, little Esther." Her mother always cooed as she laid out meagre breakfasts.

Their small house held little furniture, and their lives held little to make them glad, but for ten minutes in the morning as she held her Mother's hand, she found an oasis of happy. As they walked to the Mill they watched the peach and orange sunlight break apart the blues and greys of night; the slowly opening eye of the sky, with clouds stretching and yawning from sleep. This all gave Esther a sense of calm and happiness.

Her Mother had not smiled since Esther's Father passed away. Not a real smile, anyway; not one that reached all the way to her eyes.

"Be good. Work hard. Stay safe." Her Mother said every morning as they arrived at work, and went their separate ways.

This morning progressed as every other. The mules started their pulsing and thrashing mechanical dance, forming from the various colours of cotton thread; vast sheets of fabric.

The boys were quick to start their scavenging. They waited for the machines, with heaving arms and heavy thundering joints to move forward. In the space this presented, they flew onto their stomachs and crawled nimble as bugs under the workings. They gathered loose threads, wiped away spilled oil, and pushed out any piece of dirt that may be sat there.

Esther was not so good at timing her expeditions below the machines. This morning her timing was especially off. She waited too long on her front to be able to return to safety, and had to lay flat upon the floor, her cheek pressed hard against the cold. Arms and legs splayed out like a star, she closed her eyes and held her breath as the vibrating machine heaved itself rapidly over her. She sensed the thud of the powerful arms through the floor, felt the air move over her bare skin as metal and thread flew violently only an inch above.

Breathing slowly she waited for her moment to escape. Once the mule had retreated forward again, she found space to move, and did so with great rapidity.

"What a foozler." Sneered one of the boys.

Esther brushed herself down and waited a while before returning to the dirty work of scavenging. Her heart was racing, and her mind would not stop flashing up the sight of the dismembered body she had been forced to remove from the mule weeks before.

The foreman, thoroughly frustrated by Esther's nerves, slapped her across the back of the head.

"Back to work!"

The magpie hopped onto the window ledge, and Esther gave him the customary little salute.

"I said, back to work!"

Esther obeyed, but not before casting the man a black look.

The magpie watched as Esther returned to scavenging, and when a terrible scream rose up from one of the women working at the machines, it took flight.

The mule once again rolled over Esther, and she forced herself as flat as a pancake to avoid the crushing arms. She opened her eyes as the sound of the machine began to fade. It had not stopped as it usually did, to return over her. No. This time it continued away. The metalwork and fabric stretched tight above her continued to shake as the machine worked. She watched it slowly disappear into the distance, inexplicably further away than it should be able to reach. She dared to lift her head, and found that there was surprisingly enough room to rise onto her hands and knees.

She hurried back the way she had entered beneath the mule, but backed into rusted metalwork and piles of torn fabric. That had not been there before. She listened for the sound of the returning machine, but however much she strained, the sound became more and more distant.

She couldn't move back, so she went forward.

Here too there was rusted metalwork and torn fabric. Frustration gripped her, and she pushed her way through this obstruction. She did not want to be caught by the returning machine.

She fell forward and found herself in a cave. This deep and craggy place was a rusted and creaking scrap yard. Metal, masonry and wood in all manner of twisted shapes, corroded, aged, broken and bent formed the floor, walls and ceiling of this place. Spires of decay hung down like sword blades from the ceiling, where other, smaller daggers of the same reached up to meet them.

Esther found herself compelled to move on through this place. The air was damp and her footsteps echoed harshly. As she continued through this uneven cave, she wondered how far below the Mill she must be, and how a tunnel to this place could have opened up for her.

The thoughts were short-lived however, as a scraping sound began to register on the edge of her hearing. Short and long, drawn out and sharp, these odd noises made her pause, and hide behind a large pillar of metal and bricks.

The sounds came closer, and circled her in a flurry of tiny glinting shapes. Thimbles! Thimbles with countless hard blue legs, eyes on stalks and pincers. They swarmed around her, an array of different sizes and styles. Some thimbles were decorative and ceramic, others were cheap textured tin or copper. Esther tried to pick her feet up away from the scuttling creatures, climbing a little up the rubble at her back.

The Thimbles were laughing. They swarmed together, climbing one atop another, until they formed a great flexing mass. Esther tried to run, but slipped. The swarm reached out and formed a pincer claw, grabbing her by the ankle and lifting her into the air.

The collected creatures formed into one giant crab-like abomination. Their thousand tiny laughs combining into a roar. The roar heaved and thudded like the machines of the Mill, and Esther struggled to break free.

She hit and punched at them, pulling handfuls of the Thimbles from her leg and tossing them to the ground, where they hurried to rejoin their fellows.

Tossing her in the air, she screamed.

"*Th*top!"

Her voice rang like a gong through the cave, and the Thimble crabs shuddered. Their grip loosened, and she slipped out while still in mid air. Landing awkwardly on the uneven and hard floor winded her. She paused there, gasping for breath.

The echo faded, and the Thimbles recovered.

"Leave me alone!" She shouted when she found enough breath to do so.

Once again the echo seemed to loosen the crab's collective grip, but not by much.

"Plea*the*!"

This time the echo had much more of an effect. Why was it different this time? Was it her lisp? Thinking quickly she shouted some of the words that the teasing boys had asked her to say in recents days.

"*Th*age, *th*ack, *th*poon. *Th*illy, *th*au*th*age, *th*au*th*epan!"

It worked! The collective *th* sounds rebounded and echoed and reflected off of one another, and off of the snaggletoothed walls of the cavern. The swarm fractured and fell apart. The Thimbles clattered to the ground emitting a thousand tiny cries of protest, in the midst of which they bellowed at the girl.

"The Pin Cushion King knows you are here!"

Esther did not wait to listen to what else they had to say. She ran.

She tripped and slipped and leaped until her face was red, she was wet with sweat, and she struggled to breathe. Stopping to rest, she forced herself into hiding amongst the crags and overhangs of the cave. Tunnels branched off in multiple directions, and she had not stopped to think about turning left or right, about going up or down. She had simply run.

Now, as she slowly recovered, she listened. Nothing. Thankfully the Thimbles didn't seem to be following her. She attempted to get her bearings, and surmised that if she found tunnels that went up, she would eventually reach the surface and be able to return home, or to the Mill.

All of the branching passages looked mysteriously similar. There was no way for her to tell if she had been along any of these tunnels already. She could be walking in circles, or spirals, or back and forth.

She was becoming tired, but still she marched on, determined to find her way out of this labyrinth.

Finally she came upon an area she had not been through before. The floor dropped down in front of her in a long scree slope of iron filings and wood chips. The cave walls widened out like expanding lungs, and in this vast and cold new place she noticed little points of light. Candles. They burned together in clusters, hanging from metal chains from the craggy roof, or piled into dripping clusters on the floor.

It is now that she wondered how she had been able to see at all in these dark tunnels, with no light to see by. A distant angry voice began to echo across the cavern, and she strained to see who was speaking. Maybe she was lost in a coal mine, and had stumbled across a party of soot-covered men with pickaxes and shovels who could help her find her way home. She took one more step forward, and her weight shifted the loose ground beneath her. The top layer began to fall, then the layers below, snatching her feet from under her. Esther fell onto her back and, screaming, rode the avalanche down. Lumps and bumps and sharp things jabbed at her back, caught her dress and scratched her bare arms. Dust filled her mouth and eyes, and she choked, blinded, spitting and eyes watering.

When she eventually came to a stop, she pulled herself upright and blinked and spat and sneezed. Through watery eyes she saw the glimmer of candlelight, and the movement of someone coming close.

"Plea*th*e help me?"

She sneezed again, and wiped her eyes on the back of her hand. When she looked up now, she realised how mistaken she was to think she had come upon miners.

"You come to *my* court and dare ask for help?"

Esther gawped at the thing that stood before her. It was a large red cushion, from the top of which erupted a crown of pins, all with enamelled or jewelled heads. She backed away from the Pin Cushion King, and took in the rest of her surroundings.

In the flickering candlelight she picked out a ring of courtiers. Lords and Ladies and Dukes and Duchesses, all of them sat or slumped motionless. Through button eyes they stared at nothing. Rag dolls.

In chains to one side of her lay a magpie, and some shaggy four-legged creature all shades of brown and blue. She recognised her magpie friend from the window at the Mill.

"It'*th* you!"

"I came to find you." He said quietly, "The Pin Cushion King found me first."

The shaggy creature strained at its chains, grunting and growling. She moved towards it, but the Magpie warned her away.

"It's a ThreadBear! It'll have your hand off!"

The animal's coat was made up of threads of cotton, all matted and tangled with one another. She could only make out where the head was, by identifying which end of the creature was growling.

The Pin Cushion King jumped up and down, shouting, "This is my Kingdom now!"

He waved his thin arms at the rag dolls sat in a circle around him, commanding them to whip Esther, to punish her and to banish her. They did not move. Raging, the King kicked over the nearest doll. It flopped backward, buttons now cast at the distant dark ceiling.

Esther watched the strange and deranged Pin Cushion. She had no clue as to why he was so angry with her.

"What have I done? Why do you want to puni*th* me? I'm only a little girl!"

The Magpie tried to shush her, "Don't make him *more* angry, Princess."

Esther paused and blinked hard. What had he called her? Princess?

"Don't you call her that! Don't you dare!" The King punched and kicked at the dolls of his silent court.

The ThreadBear pulled harder at its chains, thrashing and straining. The loud sound of the King and his rage was upsetting the beast. Esther began to retreat away from it, and toward the Magpie.

The Pin Cushion King rounded on her.

"You stand upon one of the Frayed Edges of this world. When they first started to appear I tried to repair them, but now I use them."

Esther did not understand what she was hearing, but the look on the Magpie's face said all she needed to know. It was bad.

The King pulled from his crown one of the jewel ended pins. He thrust it into the floor and, wiggling it back and forth; ripped there a small hole. The Magpie tried to flap his wings, to fly away, but he could not. Chains held his wings and legs tightly. The King returned the pin to his crown, and smiled smugly.

The hole grew. From the dark space beyond this tear there appeared to be a gale blowing. The ground fluttered like fabric, which Esther knew to be impossible! It was metal and wood and brick. She could see that it was! A tearing sound accompanied the growth of the hole. It formed a long and jagged line in front of her. On one side of the tear she stood, the Pin Cushion King at her back. On the other side lay the chained Magpie and the roaring ThreadBear!

The King prodded her in the back, just as the teasing boys had done so many times.

"Jump. Or be pushed!"

He prodded her again.

"Stand up straight and pay attention to your King!"

The confusion and anger and hurt and tiredness that swilled around in her was brought suddenly to boiling point by the arrogant and goading King. She turned to him and slapped away his hand.

"No!"

The King nursed his hand, shocked by her retaliation.

"How dare you?" He hissed, "There must be something wrong with you!"

Esther vented her anger at him. She soothed her hurt by saying to him all the things she had wanted to say to the horrid teasing boys at the Mill. She let her tiredness go in a heart-thumping wave.

"I *th*all not *th*tand up *th*traight, I *th*all not do a*th* you *th*ay, and there i*th* nothing you can do to make me! There i*th* nothing wrong with me! I am perfect, ju*th*t the way I am!"

She took hold of the King by his wrist and spun him around and towards the growing tear. He teetered on the brink, balancing one way, then the other, struggling to stay upright. The storm that blew in from the other side of the Frayed Edge messed her hair and extinguished the candles. In the darkness she saw the King fall within reach of the ThreadBear, and it bit onto him. It yanked him to and fro, and as the tear grew, so the ThreadBear and the Pin Cushion King fell into the raging darkness beyond.

The Magpie flapped and fluttered, trying to pull away. The tear was coming dangerously close to him.

147

"What'*th* happening?" She asked him, shouting over the storm from the other side of the Frayed Edge.

"You need to fix the tear!"

The ground flexed once again like billowing fabric, knocking Esther on her side.

"How?" She pleaded, desperate.

Around her there was new movement. The rag doll court were beginning to stand. They pulled each other onto their well stuffed feet and advanced on the stunned girl.

One of the dolls pulled from a scabbard not a sword, but a needle. Three others moved to where the ThreadBear had been chained. Its bonds were still fixed firm, but dangled beyond the Edge. The dolls pulled at them, and heaved the ThreadBear back into the cave. They patted it and calmed it, pulling from its back one long blue thread of cotton.

The needle and the cotton were given to Esther, and she nodded. Threading the needle as quickly as she was able, she took hold of the nearest piece of the Frayed Edge, and began to sew it shut. She worked slowly, but steadily, and inch by inch the tear was fixed.

While she worked, the rag doll Lords and Ladies freed the Magpie and the ThreadBear from their chains.

"Will you help me to find my way home?" Esther asked the Magpie.

He shook his head, smiling.

"You are home. Hop on my back."

Confused, but unwilling to argue with her well-dressed friend, she climbed on his soft feathered back. He bounced forward on his nimble legs, once then twice, then with a leap and a flap they were airborne. He circled the great cavern, looking for the exit, before he began to explain.

"You are the Princess of this land. Everyone here has waited for you for a long time."
A glimmer of light caught his eye. The exit! He flapped his wings and fanned his tail, changing direction. They sped through the small opening, erupting into sudden bright, warm sunlight.

A new world unfurled around them. Flowing streams and golden hills and beautiful woods and small towns nestled at the base of a gleaming castle. The Magpie began to descend.

"The Pin Cushion King came and corrupted the Land of Threads. The Frayed Edges appeared because of him. Now that you are returned, and he is vanquished, look! See how the world is healed!"

Landing gently on a small hill, Esther slid onto the firm ground. She sat down heavily, taking in her new surroundings. Trees stood here and there with white trunks and yellow leaves. The grass beneath her fingers was brilliant green, and the sky a shade of blue she had never seen!

She rose to her feet and leant her head back, watching the strange sky. It undulated. It was not still. In the same way that a sheet rolled and curved when flung out by her mother when changing the bedding, the sky moved that same way. She held up a hand to shield her eyes from the sunlight, and squinted at the blue high above. It was silk, and running in great lines from horizon to horizon were seams covered in a million stitches.

"My name is Malachi, by the way. It is a fine day for a stroll, wouldn't you say?"

The Magpie bowed his head in formal greeting.

"I'm E*th*ther."

Malachi took her hands and shook them warmly in his feathers, "I know, Princess Esther. It is an absolute pleasure."

Together they walked through the grove of trees, where they rounded a small patchwork hill, and came upon a view of the cluster of small towns and the castle beyond. It was beautiful. It was every inch the castle from a fairy tale. Flags flew, bright banners were draped on all sides, and towers were shrouded in lush ivy.

"Who liv*th* there?"

Malachi the Magpie laughed.

"You do, of course! Come."

Esther's Mother awoke to the sound of the knocker-upper rapping on the window. She rose and dressed and prepared breakfast. She had no appetite.

She set off on the ten minute journey to the Mill, but did not make it there. She took a detour, and headed instead for the local church.

Slowly, she walked past a line of gravestones, tears welling in her eyes. She paused and rested her hand on one of the stone markers.

Lingering there for several minutes, her tears fell upon the soil, newly sprouting green shoots of grass. She sank onto her haunches, running her hands over the carved lettering of the headstone that bore her daughter's name.

THE END

ALSO AVAILABLE
by Rylan Cavell

The Department Of Lost Things
Utterly Bewildered
The Strange Adventures Of Professor Calamity

Tattoos By Rylan (a colouring book)

Printed in Poland
by Amazon Fulfillment
Poland Sp. z o.o., Wrocław